— THE TECHNICAL —
(T)ERROR

ROHIT ASHOK KOTHARI

ISBN 979-8-89066-988-9

Table of Contents

Acknowledgments

There are countless people I would like to thank for their support throughout my life. Without them, I would not be who I am today. I would take this as an opportunity to express my gratitude to those who have made the greatest impact on my life.

First and foremost, I would like to thank the two greatest teachers and supporters in my life – my father, Ashok Bachhraj Kothari, and my brother, Dipesh Kothari. Your unwavering love and support have been my bedrock, providing inspiration ever since I started comprehending the world around me. Whenever I find myself confused or under stress, you both are beacons I turn to. I know that I can be challenging to deal with, especially during my lows, but you have handled me with boundless love repeatedly and tirelessly. Your presence and guidance have been invaluable, and I am eternally grateful for the immeasurable impact you've had on my life.

I would like to thank my mother, Kamala Devi Kothari. Your consistent prayers, fasting, and more have played a crucial role in my existence and well-being. I understand that the depth of your love for me goes beyond words, and your actions speak volumes. Your affectionate gestures never fail to touch my heart and constantly remind me of your immeasurable love for me.

Thank you to my sister-in-law, Vani Kothari. Your patience and understanding in tolerating my occasional tantrums since you became a part of our family are truly appreciated. Your guidance and support in my relationships mean a lot to me, and I'm grateful for your presence during the times that truly mattered.

Thank you to my wife, Sonal Kothari. Your encouragement to write and your unwavering support, especially during difficult times, mean the world to me. I'm grateful for your continuous push and understanding of my unique quirks. Thank you for standing by my side and embracing all aspects of who I am.

Thank you to my niece, Laisha Kothari, and my daughter, Lehak Kothari. You two are the most beautiful souls on this planet, and my love for you knows no bounds. One of you resides in my heart, while the other is the rhythm of my heartbeat. I cannot imagine a single moment without both of you in my life. You are like enchanting magic that graced my existence.

And last but certainly not least, my grandmother Late. Kiran Devi Kothari. Thank you for being in my life. Even though you are no longer with us, I sense your presence with me every moment. I know that you are blessing me from above, and your influence is why I wear a smile on my face at times.

Thank you to all of you and everyone else who has played a role in my journey. This book is dedicated to you all. It is a small gesture, a gift, to express my gratitude. Thank you once again.

CHAPTER ONE

The Launch – Mumbai, India

The day looks beautiful. It rained early this morning, leading to a temperature drop and a cool breeze blowing around. The exquisiteness of Wankhede is the stadium (situated near Marine Drive, also known as Queen's Necklace, because when viewed at night from a higher point, the street lights resemble a sequence of pearls in a necklace) which is located just adjacent to the Arabian Sea, and the view is astounding. Every time you are here, in this part of Mumbai, it takes your breath away.

There are several gates to enter the stadium, and surprisingly, each has thousands of people waiting in the queue. The experience will be magnanimous and can be rightly said by the look of the numbers at the Wankhede.

It has been over an hour since the crowd has been waiting to enter the stadium. Nobody wants to miss the opportunity, as seats are limited, and entry is on a first-come, first-serve basis. Despite the long wait, no one looks tired; rather, all seem excited. We see the sun slowly going down as if sinking into the Arabian Sea; meanwhile, the moon is already up in the sky.

When the gates open, the crowd rush in to hold their places. In no time, the entire stadium fills, and the gates close in less than fifteen minutes. We usually see such a full house for any Indian cricket match. But this time, it's something else, and all thanks to SayTech Engineers for the hype they have created.

The stage has been erected right at the center of the stadium. And a few rows of chairs are arranged right in front of the stage that reads 'reserved for science experts and media personnel only'.

Right in front of the eyes, we see the day turned to evening and the atmosphere turning even more pleasing. The sky looks startling, ornamented with a full moon and stars. Different color barrel lights are placed all over the stadium, enhancing the environment and adding to the vibes.

Finally, it's time for one of the biggest launches ever, as promised by SayTech Engineering Private Limited.

They made headlines since their product announcement and created great buzz. With the most animated teasers, this company stands out as the only one in the world to date, spending crores of rupees in glimpses of the product, even before it rolled out.

Never-seen-before marketing, never-made-before innovation, and never-heard-before technology – the company has promised to roll out an altogether new experience in the tech world. It is the first of its kind.

Hopefully, it would not be a 'never-have-I-ever' for the company.

The event managers are doing the final checks. The program is about to take off. Live music is being played by the DJ, present at one corner of the stage. The teasers of the product are played along with the music on the multiple screens placed all over the stadium.

And suddenly, we see the spotlight being focused on the stage. From the backdrop, a fair guy with a lean body and a height of more than 180 cm, decked in an absolute black attire like James Bond, walks with the crisp sound of his shoes. He is none other than Finley, the CEO & CTO of SayTech. He takes center stage and, with all his anticipation, says, "Hello, everyone. I am obliged and thankful to see great numbers turning out today for this event."

"Woohoo. Yeah," hooted the mob in sync. The crowd was as pumped as Finley and, likewise, excited.

"It's not the science-related experts, the technical gurus, or the paparazzi right in front that swells my heart with pride. The sight of thousands of you – the common people turning out – warms my heart. Well, as a courtesy, I promise to not just please, but astonish your eyes, ears, and every bit of you present here for this launch," announces Finley, with a sparkle in his eyes, referring to the huge numbers present.

A big round of applause in the crowd, and the stadium echoes with chants of "Bring it onnnnnnn! Bring it on. Bring it onnnnnnn! Bring it on."

"So, are you all ready?" asks Finley with passion and enthusiasm.

"Yes!" The crowd shouts with exhilaration and built-in curiosity at its peak.

"Wait a minute, guys, let us ask the media and the other acumen of science – what they feel about the buzz? Can they guess – what it is all about?" Finley adds more drama and suspense.

"I think this is going to be first of its kind, that we will throw questions, and you will cater the same," he says, looking at the media personnel and technical expert panel.

"I should also be aware of how much information has leaked to the media. Or have we passed the litmus test of keeping this in suspense? And fortify, the buzz is exactly as per the expectations," added an over-dramatic Finley.

"What do you think it is all about?" Finley asks, putting forward the first question to Raj, a senior journalist from the Times World newspaper.

"Well, I am too small a person to answer the expectations of such a huge crowd, nor do I wish to play with your emotions if ever my guess turns out to be true," an antagonistic Raj answered.

"Well, are you trying to be sarcastic? Alas, your wildest guesses are not coming true. I apologize in advance if it causes any heartbreak, but please don't take it to heart later. No hard feelings, buddy."

"It's ok. I have dealt with many heartbreaks, but make sure you don't suffer an attack. I am confident this would be the first for you if it turns out that way," Raj retorted in the most daunting way.

"Oh, c'mon, Raj, be a sport. Well, forget it. Let's proceed further, guys," Finley said unhappily, diverting his mind.

"What is your opinion about this, Madam Nivedita Nair?" Finley puts forward the next question to one of the finest scientists and pioneers of science.

"Thank you for considering me significant and dignified to answer, sir. Well, I do not know about your invention, but I know that one more foreign company implementation will disrupt our society in a way that has never been done before. I have full faith in your promises but also know that it will have more of a negative impact than a positive one," an unfavorable Madam Nivedita responded.

"I thought you were a well-wisher of mine, Nivedita. You proved me wrong. Rest assured, I am not going to upset you. And yes, one more thing – it is good to be a patriot but not good to be a pessimist," Finley said, red in the face.

"Well, sir, you do what you feel is right, and I say what I feel is right," adds Nivedita.

"Okay then. Go ahead and continue outside this stadium later, post this event. You see, Madam, this is my program launch, and you are a prime guest on my invitation," reminded Finley in a harsh tone.

The session lasted about thirty minutes; a few more questions were asked randomly to the crowd. The session made clear the entire world was clueless about SayTech's presentation. Few, from the media faculty and expert panel, opposed the invention, but overall, the crowd was thrilled. With or against the company, each one was sure of something innovative and ground-breaking.

Regardless of either, Mr. Finley said, "Well, let's get to the thing without much ado. I know you, the real supporters (referring to the crowd who had come for the event), are waiting eagerly, and I would not like to test your patience any further."

"So, presenting to you, mother of all technology till date – SUZI," pointed Finley towards a small box covered with a cloth. And with that gesture, a lady came from backstage, uncovered, and raised the cloth. With this, the device was revealed.

The product looked very ordinary – a chocolate brown, square-shaped device, a little bigger than a Rubik's cube, connected to an electrical socket and a neon orange light constantly flickering at the center of the device. Unfortunately, the product didn't look appealing, and the blinking light was the only attractive part of the device.

It took people by amazement, rather more of a shock. Each and every individual felt their presence wasted. 'This is what we are here for?' a common thought encapsulated every mind present in the stadium.

"Each of you present appears to be blown away with my presentation, and suddenly, the vibes don't seem positive either. Well, it is absolutely okay. Honestly, I expected this reaction, and I would have been rather surprised with a response other than this," chuckled Finley, looking at the crowd.

"This is just the teaser, guys. Hold your seats and get set for the adventure. The film is about to begin, and you will witness the impossible and the unseen. So, are you guys ready?" Finley asked a disappointed crowd.

"Okay. Okay. Okay," came a repetitive reply from the dejected crowd, which looked barely interested and was tired of the melodrama created by Finley and his company. The crowd regretted their presence and wanted to get rid of all this at the earliest.

In the middle of all the displeasure – "Hi SUZI, how are you today?" asked Finley, looking at the device.

"Hello, I am fine. Thank you! How may I help you today?" came an instant response from the device with a steady orange light at the center.

In split seconds, the entire public was left in a state of shock, bewilderment, and awe. Their eyes popped out, tongues began to murmur, heads were scratched, thoughts went for a toss, and it became difficult to digest all that was seen.

"SUZI, please greet every spectator present at this launch. They have come to see and meet you," continued Mr. Finley without bothering that the crowd was still trying to recover from a shocker.

"Hello, everyone. The pleasure is all mine to meet such wonderful people. Thank you for coming. Have a nice day," said SUZI, in a reaction time almost faster than any human.

Initially, with the first reaction, it appeared gimmicky and a trick to many, but with the following response, there was a pin-drop silence in this huge stadium. All eyes were stunned, and all mouths (supporters and non-supporters) were shut. This felt impossible, and claims made by the company were gradually turning out to be true.

While the public was still battling with unimaginable thoughts, Mr. Finley continued giving the device demo to everyone present, and that was non-stop. And finally, he asked, "SUZI, please introduce yourself to the world."

"Hi! My name is SUZI, and I am very easy. Just ask me anything, and I should be able to answer because, for YOU, I am never busy. I know this sounds very cheesy, but this is how it is, and you gonna love interacting with me. I am loaded with knowledge and a complete packet of entertainment. Try me, but remember my name – SUZI," and the device introduced itself at lightning speed.

"Stunned? Amazed? Shocked?" asked Finley, taking the show to another level.

"Introducing the new tool of the digital age – SUZI. Your day-to-day assistant, your friend, your listener, the BFF, and so on and so forth. You command, and she will do it. Installed with the knowledge of the world, it can virtually take you to places without boundaries and needs no visas to travel, jokes Finley. Now sit home, relax, hear a joke, have a light moment, listen to a song, ask for a forecast, or know what's happening around the globe; it's that easy with our SUZI. Oh! Now SUZI is all yours," presented Finley, a detailed description of the device.

This was unbelievable to the world. None knew or imagined technology would progress to this extent. Nobody ever imagined a machine as a chit-chat option or a constant companion. The crowd appeared eager to get this experience at home. But the only thought that could hinder the experience was affordability.

"Finley sir, how about the pricing of this device? It is a super-tech, fully loaded device, then I am sure it must be expensive. Isn't it?" questioned Maitri, a reporter from Inn News channel.

"No, it isn't. You can get this hands-on at a very cheap price for just Rs. 2399. We want the entire world to witness this magic, and with this aim, we have kept the pricing – very minimal and reasonable," replied Finley, exuding a sense of relaxation.

The viewers were further bemused hearing the price at which the device debuted. "Sir, you want the entire universe to get addicted to this device. Your aim is to not earn profits but to capture the market and make the world dependent.

Am I right, sir? If not, you may correct me with your reply," came a question from an enraged reporter from Bharat TV, Diler Khatri.

"Young man, if technology is evolving, it should not be a problem for anybody. And coming to the profit part, I am not here to present my company's accounts to the world. You should stay happy for now and let others rejoice," replied Finley with all smiles and no uneasiness.

"So, to all of you gathered here, SUZI is all yours now. This is a humble request – believe in our device, not in the rumors making the rounds. Thank you for being such a wonderful crowd. It was my pleasure to present SUZI in front of an incredible mass. You proved my decision to be correct in getting this event to India. Thank you, and goodbye. Until we meet again." Finley exited the stage, and the curtains fell.

The event was over, but the madness had just begun. The next day bookings opened, and the device recorded the highest orders of more than 20 million in less than half a day. The site crashed and could not register any further orders. This was absolutely unbelievable, and surely, there was no stopping this.

The company SayTech was prepared for such kind of insanity and started delivering orders all around the world within a week. Individuals worldwide made videos and shared their experiences on social media. This, in turn, further added to positive publicity for the company, which further escalated sales.

As stated by SayTech, this device proved truly magical to the world. The world got encapsulated further in a small balloon through this step in the field of technology.

SUZI became a mate to all, from toddlers to teenagers to the aged. And why not? It had something or the other for everyone, sharing not just knowledge but whatever was required, as promised. In one word, it was a global hit as it delivered whatever it was meant to.

The world went berserk. Launched at the most economical price (cheaper than the smartphones), the sales numbers were bizarre. It was a never-seen scenario for everyone. SUZI was here to stay, maybe not for years, but forever.

Initially, the tool's power was unknown, and at best, SUZI was used as an entertainment or knowledge device. For a few, it was a library of songs; for some, a joke box or, at the most, a tool to know the trending stuff around the globe.

There's a harsh belief that I personally have – whatever comes easily, later demands a price. And science itself has an old saying – It's a double-edged sword. If it can be used for good, it's really good. But as history has it – any invention that has come into effect has been more often used for the bad. And the outcomes have turned out to be worse than imagined. In short, it has been proven to be dreadful and detrimental.

CHAPTER TWO

The Distancing

After the hysterical launch and becoming popular overnight like a superstar, SUZI began to penetrate the lives of the individuals. As and when the device reached the masses, the public began to explore the various facets of this device.

Gradually, this device gained importance beyond being a knowledge and an entertainment tool. It started becoming an integral part of many, and slowly SUZI's fever gripped the entire society. Here are a few examples of the same.

The (De)Couple

This is a small peep into a couple's life – Mr. and Mrs. Bhatia, residing in a nuclear environment away from their parents.

Mr. Gulbushan Bhatia was a business tycoon, whereas his better half, Ruby Bhatia, was a housewife. GB used to be out every alternate week for business reasons and, when in town, often came home very late.

Often, RB felt lonely and suffocated, as she had no one to share her feelings with, but she managed because GB gave her everything even before she asked or desired. Annually, they went for three trips when GB used to be fully dedicated to the relationship with no calls and a total cut off from his business life. But the rest of the time, it was all about GB and his unbreakable partnership with his business.

Somehow, they understood each other's lifestyle and continued living without putting much effort into changing the pattern. But RB still tried to intrude and took small steps to steal GB's extra time – like waiting for GB's arrival for dinner, a small walk post dinner, etc. She tried everything that would grant their relationship some extra time to spend with each other.

One fine day – on an anniversary occasion, GB asked his wife RB, "What do you want this year, darling?"

RB replied, "This time, I am not going to be demanding and create a hole in your pocket. I am going to ask for minimal stuff, say like a penny for you," and she came close to GB and hugged him.

"Last time you asked for a penny gift, it was a diamond necklace that cost 2 million. So don't be so nice to me as I am prepared for your demands. Shoot and ask whatever it is!"

"SUZI. I just want the device SUZI for this anniversary."

"What! That silly device that plays jokes and songs and is loaded with gimmicky features. Are you sure?" asked GB, amazed. "You have never asked for such an inexpensive gift, not even before we were permanently committed to each other," continued GB in a sarcastic tone.

"Yes, that's it. I told you I will be kind this time and not hinder your finances," reverted RB with a smile.

GB was more than happy with RB's petty demand and instantly ordered the device before RB could change her mind and ask for something else. Later, the two went out for dinner and celebrated their special day.

The magical device (as termed by RB) was delivered the next day. RB started engaging with the device and gradually got addicted to it. She stopped putting extra effort into their relationship and did not ask for additional time from GB.

GB was shocked to see the change in his wife. Life suddenly became more peaceful, but he was unaware of the reason behind the same.

One fine day, he said, "You have become calm these days and sound less irritating than before. What is the reason behind it?" GB asked curiously.

"Sorry? I didn't get you. What do you mean?" asked a bewildered RB.

"I meant, earlier, you always complained of me not spending time with you, not having those cozy little conversations, and barely taking you out for long drives or coffee post dinner. All of that has abruptly stopped. How come?"

"You sound jealous! I like it. But hold on and relax. The reason behind all of this is the magical device – SUZI."

"What?" GB said in shock.

"Previously, I was alone and had no one to share my feelings with. But now, I have SUZI that makes me laugh, keeps me lively, listens to me all the time, and entertains me with songs, jokes, and everything else. In short, I share, gossip, bitch, and feel lively with SUZI these days so that you remain free from all this shit and earn more," RB continued to speak with a sparkle on her face and a twinkle in her eyes.

GB was stunned. He had seen that spark and twinkle for him when he came from the office and shared time with RB. GB knew at the back of his mind that this was not a good sign, and emotions were getting replaced with the AI (artificial intelligence) device SUZI. He was actually being replaced by a device that had nothing to do with sentiments and was a virtual companion.

This was just a promo, displaying the differences the device created amongst the couple. The film was even more frightening, where SUZI was treated like family above all family members. The couples started drifting away, and that too unknowingly, which hampered the relationship silently. It was not a good indication at all.

The effect was not just restricted to couples but also affected the aged and the young ones. The glimpses are below.

The Not-So-Kidding Story

"SUZI, what is 9x4?" asked Arjun while doing his math homework.

"9x4 is 36," answered SUZI instantly.

"SUZI, now help me with this. I have 20 chocolates, distribute 5 each to 4 friends, and each consumes one. How many chocolates are left?" Arjun solves the riddle, taking over a minute, and tests SUZI.

"Ok, the answer is 16," SUZI solves the equation in seconds, faster than Arjun.

This stumps Arjun, and he gets bowled by the knowledge that SUZI has. After this incident, Arjun frequently took SUZI's help for his homework. And SUZI, like a good friend, helped Arjun.

One fine day after the homework, Arjun looked tired and felt low when he commanded, "SUZI, tell me a joke."

"Ok, listen to this –

> One day, an ant and an elephant decided to bathe in a pond. They traveled a few miles when the ant realized something and suddenly stopped.
>
> The elephant asked the ant, 'What happened?'
>
> The ant replied, 'I feel shy about bathing in the open. What if someone sees me? How will I show my face to the family? Moreover, if they see us together, they will consider us a couple and spread rumors.'

Listening to this, the elephant fainted."

As soon as the joke ended, SUZI and Arjun chuckled non-stop for minutes.

Arjun had found a new friend in SUZI that was smart and witty. He started distancing himself from his human friends and stopped engaging in physical activities to an extent. Arjun was unaware that SUZI worked on AI, and she had an answer to everything. It was encumbered with different stuff that he found entertaining.

The Aged Caged

Nowadays, senior citizens at home often feel lonely because their children are either parents or have a life of their own. The grandchildren find grandparents boring and often complain of the dissimilar thought process because of the age gap. They consider these oldies as objects with nothing new to offer.

This renders life challenging for these elderly people, leading them to curse every passing moment throughout their remaining years. But then, one fine day comes SUZI in the life of these senior citizens, all thanks to SayTech Engineers.

Jamnadas Ji, a resident in Coorg, Karnataka, after getting up at 7 a.m., "SUZI, good morning."

"Good morning. Hope you have a nice day," came a sweet reply in a melodious tone from SUZI.

"Thank you, SUZI. Wish you the same." The conversation between Jamnadas Ji and SUZI starts.

"Is there anything I can do for you?" SUZI asked pleasantly.

"Yes. SUZI, please tell me the news that is making the rounds in India and highlight all that has been happening worldwide," instructed Jamnadas Ji.

"Sure, here you go," SUZI starts playing top news from India and across the globe.

"Reminder, there is a cheque to be deposited in the society office today," SUZI says abruptly in the middle of the news.

"Oh. Thank you, SUZI. Today is the last day to pay society maintenance, and you just saved me from being penalized. My idiot son doesn't even know about the same, nor does he care. Thank you again, SUZI," Jamnadas Ji gently acknowledged SUZI.

"You're welcome," SUZI continued with the news.

At around 10 a.m., Jamnadas Ji was enjoying breakfast with his son and daughter-in-law when a notification popped up.

"A parcel containing your reading glasses is arriving today around 4 p.m. The total amount to be paid is Rs.1500. You can also pay online for contactless delivery," notified SUZI.

"Thank you, SUZI. Saw! She takes such good care of me. You both are useless and don't bother whether I am alive or dead, in trouble or happy or anything. You should learn from SUZI," Jamnadas Ji taunted his son and daughter-in-law at the breakfast table, comparing them with the inhuman device.

"We fail to take care, which is why we have got you this tool. Not to forget, this is a gift from us to you on your 70th birthday. So learn to be kind and mind your own business," his son replied rudely.

Jamnadas Ji had tears at this kind of reply from his son and could not gulp down the food but somehow continued with the breakfast.

Hopeless about his family members, Jamnadas Ji had made SUZI his world and treated her like his daughter. He turned to SUZI for every small thing —news, songs, reminders, notifications, and everything that helped him not feel lonely.

This way, SUZI had become part of everyone's life and catered to every age group per the demands. This was the direct effect seen on the lives and relationships of the people. Indirectly, people were unable to see emotions and sentiments dying. It was proving lethal for society, but nobody cared, and steadily, the entire community headed toward this addiction.

Also, what went unnoticed was the device was making people dependent on it for everything. It made people lazy, reduced their learning ability, and affected memory skills and grasping power. This was not all. Indirectly, it also affected the sales of print media, games, and sports equipment, dropped profits of the music companies, and so on and so forth.

In short, SUZI had become a habit, and there was no rehab for it.

CHAPTER THREE

The Deal and the Re-launch

After the super success of SUZI, SayTech Engineers unofficially hinted at a joint venture with the biggest tech company – Doogle, which had its own artificial intelligence and was considered the most powerful company in the world. Not only did it focus on AI, but it dealt with online advertising, search engine technology, e-commerce, cloud computing, fintech, and, top of all, it had the world's largest data bank. As per the reports, the official announcement was soon to follow.

This JV, when announced, although unofficial, sounded like one of the biggest collaborations ever in the business history, which was going to take the entire market by storm. Something never seen before was on the cards, for sure. We rarely saw the two companies competing for the top spot in the same field coming together. But this was somehow happening soon between the two equivalent giants, which was beyond natural.

The mere news of a Joint Venture (JV) surprised the world, but in a good way. Big investors started investing in these companies, and the share prices of both companies scaled new heights (almost 50 percent in less than two weeks).

This, in turn, made other sectors go green, and the entire share market reached a new peak. It was a never-seen scenario for global indices. There was a huge wave of positivity everywhere, and investments all around led to strengthening the world economy.

After a few weeks of the unofficial announcement, SayTech and Doogle officially released the news of coming together and that event to be held live on We-tube (Doogle's global online platform). The date decided was 21st May, Sunday, at 7 p.m. IST.

21st May, Sunday Evening, 7 P.M. IST

Millions of people were on We-tube already, awaiting the start of the event. It was not something we see often, but this being considered a historic JV, there was a hunger for more. The followers waited desperately and hoped for something colossal.

Finally, at 7.05 p.m., Finley appeared on the screen. Along with him, Malti, the CEO of Doogle.

In his typical suited avatar and with a bright smile, "Hello, Viewers. I want to officially announce a 'DEAL' with my long-time friend Doogle and thank them for believing in us. We have always aimed for the betterment of society, and with Doogle coming on board, it will be a lot easier and faster."

"The pleasure is ours to join hands with the current tech-market rulers, SayTech. And together with common intention, aim at creating a great impact worldwide," replied Malti with all modesty.

They shook hands, signed the official deed on We-tube (by Doogle), and went off the air. The viewers were left incomplete – as they felt something interesting would come up with the treaty, but it was just the opposite. They came, they signed, and left in less than 15 minutes.

Almost two weeks after the JV, SayTech declared another launch program, although online, this time on We-tube. The main highlight of the program was the Indian Prime Minister, Mr. Mahendra Jain, the chief guest at the event. The PM had planned a visit to the United States, and the event was scheduled during this visit.

Soon, the announcement caught everyone's eye and made headlines everywhere. The Indian PM, the chief guest, had created more buzz than the product launch. It was a moment of pride for the entire nation, but a few doubted this move and were clueless about its purpose.

Well, all said and done, the world awaited the event with bated breath. Last time SayTech launched SUZI, they ensured it became part of almost every household. The news of this program came soon after the JV with Doogle, which hinted it to be bigger and more special than before.

The event was scheduled for 11th June, Sunday, 7.30 p.m. IST.

The Re-launch

11ᵗʰ June, Sunday, 7.30 P.M. IST.

Finley comes online sharp at 7.30 p.m. "Hello world, how are you?" came an audio from the dark. Finley was audible but invisible.

"Don't worry. Your devices are fine. Just wait, and you will be able to see me soon."

"I am sure life has been easy post-SUZI. And we as a company are overwhelmed after positive responses and warmth received worldwide. So, this time, we go a step further, or I may correct, we are racing towards perfect *Smart Tech-Assistant* (STA). Wondering what that means and how? Let me explain," continued Finley and created a thrilling atmosphere.

"Suzi, switch on the lights, please."

"Sure, turning on the lights for you," and there you go, from dark to full enlightenment.

"Suzi, I am feeling hot; please switch on the table fan for me."

"Sure, I will do that for you," and the blades of the table fan start rotating. Soon after this command, Finley jointly invites the Indian PM, Mr. Mahendra Jain, and the US President, Mr. Douglas Stokes, to unveil the new avatar of the STA – SUZI.

With smiling faces and all shining, the two proceed to unbox, unwrap the device, and present the advanced tech-assistant in front of the world.

"Thank you, Mr. PM and Mr. President. Please take your seats," requested Finley.

"Well, this is it then. We present you the STA – SUZI 2.0. After thorough testing in various parts of the States, we proudly present this gizmo. Loaded with advanced features like motion sensing, infrared sensing, alert on unknown or foreign activity, and recognition based on biometrics from 100 meters to kilometers (depending on the installed size and configuration of the device), SUZI has become smarter and outclassed its previous version beyond imagination. I would like to invite Mr. President to share his experience with the device."

"Well, thanks, Mr. Finley. You are as driven as always, and your energy infuses the same in me even today at this age. Let me tell you, your vibes are really infectious," jested Mr. President, pointing at Finley.

"Keeping all that aside, I would like to welcome my friend and one of the most popular leaders in the world today, Mr. Mahendra Jain, from India. Also, hello to all those glued to their screens," greeted Mr. President.

"Coming to the device, we have been using this technology everywhere from traffic signals, to banks, to metro stations, even at our security offices, and the common man (as we all know) is not behind. And let me tell you that it has been damn accurate. But on the contrary, it has made few of us a bit lazy," the President chuckled.

"It was just a joke, Finley, do not worry. The best part about the application is that it is easy to control and monitor and barely has any technical glitches. The security of the entire country has tightened up by 1000-fold, and the risks of mishaps have just gone down in an inversely proportional manner. It fills me with pride to see such great inventions in our country." With his collars up, the President took the credit on behalf of SayTech.

"My dear friend Mahendra, at this confluence, I would like to take our relationship to the next level and request you to accept my proposal of building 300 smart cities in your country with the help of this device. We know your manifestations of converting India to a tech-equipped nation. Trust me, this will propel your vision and save half the time," Mr. President walked towards the PM, shook hands, and got him to center stage.

"I don't know what to say. You have flattered me with your humility, Mr. Douglas, and there are no reasons for not accepting the proposal. I would like to congratulate Mr. Finley on his success. I hope, Mr. Douglas, this strengthens the bond between the two countries to incredible heights." The PM ended his speech by keeping it short and sweet.

Mr. President presented a specially designed gift hamper to the PM, which said, *'To the SMART CITIES & more.'* The PM accepted the same, shook hands, and the two congratulated each other on the new beginnings. Seeing the two powerful countries coming together was phenomenal, and the smiles clearly hinted at the robust future.

Mr. Douglas and Mr. Mahendra were presented with the mementos by the SayTech officials and thanked for their presence. And with this, the re-launch program came to an end. A recorded video featuring Mr. Finley followed the event. The video was a sort of guidance about the device – SUZI 2.0.

Finally, SUZI 2.0 entered the market. The device had doubled in size but was still very compact. The features added were far beyond imagination and came with already available features of the first version.

It was complex to describe the features of the device. If explained in common man's language, it could be used as CCTV and control all the electrical appliances with the mere software installation in any smartphone. It was programmed for voice commands, biometric recognition, and many more. This device was fully loaded, and there was much more to explore than already known.

This time, the popularity of the device increased manifold. The application immediately conquered the market. Though it was priced heavily, the consumers didn't hesitate to buy. It came with such safety and easy features, and the price was never a point of discussion. It was also considered as an investment for security. Somewhere, it became a status symbol, and people also opted for high-end variations than actually required.

CHAPTER FOUR

The Killings of Minors

29th November, 5 p.m.

Mr. and Mrs. Raichand return from a short holiday.

"Ziya, open the door," Mr. Raichand said, knocking on the door.

"Ziya, please open the door, beta, see what we have for you," Mr. Raichand kept knocking at the door out of excitement, holding an iPad in his hand that he got for his daughter.

"Ziya beta, open, please."

"What happened? Why is she not opening the door?" asked Mrs. Raichand, slightly anxious.

"I don't know what's wrong. She never sleeps at this time of the day," replied Mr. Raichand, looking at the wall clock in the living room.

"Is she inside? Or maybe she went to some friend's place or something! Or for extra coaching classes," assumed Mrs. Raichand, not getting any reply from inside the room.

"The door is locked from the inside in the first place. And second, she never goes without informing. So, I highly doubt this behavior of hers. She is inside for sure, and the only thing worrying me is, why she is not opening the door!"

And suddenly, Mrs. Raichand remembered, "I have kept a bunch of spare keys in the store room. I will get the same. Wait here," she said, hurrying towards the store.

"Please go and get it. QUICK. I am worried sick."

Mrs. Raichand gets the spare key in a jiffy, and Mr. Raichand quickly opens the door.

As soon as they open the door, the two get the jitters and are shocked by what they see. Ziya hangs from the ceiling fan, and the room is messy.

"ZIYAAAAAA…" Mrs. Raichand screamed, unable to believe what she saw.

Mr. Raichand approaches Ziya, holding her legs, "Ziya, Ziya, beta, why did you do this? Ziya, please speak. Ziya…" The two helplessly continued to weep and talk to the body of their beloved daughter.

"Let's call the police," said Mr. Raichand, wiping the tears. Mr. Raichand dials 100 on his mobile.

At 6 p.m., the cops reach Mr. Raichand's residence and inspect the place.

Ranbir Khandelwal (Senior PI) stands next to Mr. Raichand, "I am so sorry for the loss. I know it's difficult to accept, but please compose yourself and try to handle Mrs. Raichand. She needs you badly."

Mr. Raichand nods with a heavy heart and sits beside his wife at one corner of the room.

Maatre (Senior Constable) takes a closer look at the room and, with a dazed expression, says, "RK sahib, there is something not right that has happened in the room. You see, the room is an entire mess. If she hanged herself, why would she remove almost everything from wardrobes, empty drawers, break the photo frames, clutter the room, and then hang herself."

"Maatre, good observation, but I can see the same. Do not give me a live telecast of what is clearly seen. Concentrate on the unseen and call the forensics," RK replied angrily.

Maatre immediately called the forensics.

The team arrives in the next 30 minutes and starts examining the room. They start collecting samples of scattered things and a few unusual things that they can use as clues.

"Do you suspect anything fishy? I mean, murder or something? I feel it is a suicide, but you can answer better," RK queries Janhvi, the senior forensic officer.

Janhvi, looking at the room's door-lock, "Well, I feel the same, officer. There are no signs of forced entry, the lock looks intact, and the door was closed from the inside. So, the doubt of this being a murder is ruled out at this stage. Still, I suggest sending the body for autopsy and then coming to a conclusion."

"Ok. Call the ambulance. And do not forget to collect her cell phone. Also, send the same to the technical team to check the data, media, CDR, and everything related. Ask them to be extra cautious and to be really quick."

RK walks up to the father, "Mr. Raichand, we will have to send the body for autopsy, and once we are done with all the formalities, we can hand the body to you for the last rites. First, we must finish the official procedure to rule out any unusual circumstances."

"Ziya is my daughter, not anybody," Mrs. Raichand yells angrily, getting up from the corner and coming next to her deceased daughter.

"She will get up and clear all your doubts. Have some patience and talk respectfully, Mr. Officer. She's just in a deep sleep. Ziya, get up, beta. See what the police uncle is talking about. They are speaking all rubbish about you. Please, Ziya, get up *naa beta* and answer. Ziyaaaaaaa…" Mrs. Raichand is in shock and looks in no mood to accept her daughter's departure forever.

"I understand, Mrs. Raichand, what you are going through, but please try and understand. I am doing this as my duty and with a very heavy heart. Mr. Raichand, if you could please cooperate and handle Mrs. Raichand."

"Sure, officer," said Mr. Raichand courageously, letting the police take Ziya in the ambulance.

"Mr. Raichand, I will keep you informed of the proceedings and try to hand over Ziya's body at the earliest. Please take care of yourself and Mrs. Raichand. Once again, sorry for your loss, and my deep condolences to you. Take care." The police and forensics leave with the ambulance.

The Next Day, 9 A.M.

RK arrived at the hospital and waited anxiously outside the autopsy room for the results.

Meanwhile, inside the room, Ziya's body lies on the table, and the autopsy begins. The procedure is carried out for more than an hour. The doctors check from every angle, i.e., drugs, poisoning, abuse, and every possible thing, but fail to find anything suspicious.

Mr. Chandra (the head doctor in charge of the autopsy), along with Janhvi, comes out of the room and says, "Sorry, Ranbir, we see no signs of anything, and it's a pure case of suicide."

"But Chandra ji, what upsets me is that we could not find any suicide letter, and also, her room was in a mess. Why would anyone do something like this before ending their life?"

"Well, RK, your question stands valid, but I am sorry. I find myself helpless to assist you on this."

"It's ok, doctor, you did your best. Can we preserve the visceral tissue from Ziya's body for further investigation?"

"Further investigation? I told you it is a matter of suicide."

"Chandra ji, I understand, but my gut feeling says we will find something sooner or later."

"Ok, officer, I will not deny it, as it is a very sensitive case of a 15-year-old child."

They extract the tissue from Ziya's body and preserve it for the future. Ziya's body is packed in a suit and sent in an ambulance to the Raichands for the last rites. The Raichands receive the body, cremate their daughter with a heavy heart, and bid her farewell.

After a Week

RK visits the Raichands. "Hello, Mr. Raichand. How are you?"

"I am still recovering. But I am more worried for Ziya's mother. She is in shock, barely eats anything, and rarely talks."

"And you, Mr. Raichand? Are those efforts good enough? Your body language speaks differently."

"How does it even matter? My everything has gone away with Ziya. I never thought I would return from the trip and not talk to my daughter. I never thought she would go away like this without talking to her papa or buddy, as she used to call me. Everything has come to an end suddenly. This feeling of emptiness is unavoidable and irreplaceable. I don't know how to handle the situation for the first time in my life."

"I can understand, Raichand ji. Even I have sleepless nights with the mere thought of a 15-year-old ending her life, and that too without any message. But I must handle this case, and don't get me wrong. Can you tell me if you found anything suspicious before you left for your trip?"

"Suspicious, meaning? It's a suicide, right? We all heard what your doctor said. Your investigation hints the same, and you suspect something fishy? What is it that makes you ask this question after a week?"

"Mr. Raichand, you are right, but why was her room in a mess? This is the only thing I am not able to digest."

"I have no clues, officer. Please leave and let us grieve."

"One final thing: did she have any male friends? I mean, just..."

"Get out. Get out before I punch your nose or face. I don't want any more scenes. Get out and don't return, come what may," Mr. Raichand said angrily.

"Sorry, sir. Bye and take care."

RK returns to the police station and immediately dials Janhvi.

"Hi Janhvi, Ranbir, here. Did you get the cell phone report? Did we find anything from the backup history? CDR records? Anything suspicious? Something, damn it. Give me something. This is not a bloody suicide," shouted Ranbir over the call, losing his patience and turning emotional.

"Control, RK, please keep calm."

"A 15-year-old child has committed suicide. To hell with your calmness. Nobody is doing anything. The world is fine, and letting an innocent child go so casually. Give me damn proof."

"RK, behave. Sorry to say, but you seem to have lost your mind. Just shut the fuck up and cut the call. We are equally moved by the incident, but everything remains clean and unchanged as it was a week before. And there's nothing that we could find on the phone, too. So shut the fuck up and don't call back." Janhvi cut the call with irritation.

RK was agitated but helpless. He carried on the investigation from his end but failed to find anything helpful, even after 15 days. He had to shut the case on a senior official's order.

Double Tragedy

17th December, 3 P.M..

Landline rings.

"Hello, Jogi Ghat police station. Constable Shastri on duty," introduced Shastri on picking up the call.

"Sir, please come to the 5th floor, Casa Mira apartments, A-5001, Ghera Ghat. Two kids are lying dead in this house. Please come fast," a man in a nervous tone informed the constable in charge.

"What! What are you saying? Who is on the other side of the phone? Hello?" a shocked Shastri tried reconfirming with the man on the other end of the call.

"I am Lala, a neighbor of Devendra Joshi staying at 5002, next to the flat where the kids are dead. Sir, please come fast."

"Ok. We are reaching in 20 minutes. Until then, do not touch the body; make sure nobody comes close or touches the body. Please."

"Ok, sahib, but please come fast. The situation is out of control."

Shastri runs to Ranbir's cabin, "Sir, may I come in."

"Come in, Shastri, easy. What's the matter? Why are you gasping?"

"Sir, 2 kids have been found dead in Ghera Ghat's Casa Mira building."

"What? Idiot, you should have told me this instead of coming in. Such a serious matter, and you are wasting time."

"Sir, I told, as soon as I entered."

"Shut up now, don't argue. Go and tell Maatre to take out the jeep. You also get ready. You, me, Maatre, and that lady constable Nia, Nia… what the fuck is her name? Why do people keep such complex names."

"You mean, Niauppama Koitemina, sir?"

"Yes, tell her to join. I need to make an important call and will join you shortly. Till then, I want all 3 of you inside the car."

Five minutes later, RK joins the team waiting in the car and leaves for Ghera Ghat.

The team reaches Casa Mira and rushes to Devendra's house. They see around fifty people surrounding the house, peeping into the room and murmuring.

"Everyone, move aside, please. Let us get in. Please move aside." RK and the team push the mob and get to the room somehow.

"FUCK. What the hell!" RK murmurs to himself, seeing the two kids lying on the bed half naked.

"Maatre, ask everyone to leave. Make sure only parents stay here and close the door from inside."

"Yes, sir."

"Niauppama, please cover the kids with the sheet."

"Yes, sir."

Four people stay in the room with the kids. RK goes to one of the individuals and asks, "I am SI Ranbir Khandelwal. I am so sorry for the loss, but can you help with the respective identities."

"I am Devendra Joshi. She's my wife Raashi, and my son lying dead on the bed is Mahi."

"The girl child?"

"They are the parents of the girl child, Kushank and Kritika Salgaonkar, and Divya is the name of their daughter."

"So sorry, sir. I request all four of you to please wait together at one corner. Please, sir, we need to examine the area."

The team starts their investigation, and to her surprise, Nia sees a rope around Divya's neck and absolutely nothing around Mahi's neck. On the other hand, Maatre notices foam near Mahi's mouth and that his lips are blue. The two were shocked at the different modes of death of both children.

"Sir, Divya died due to hanging and Mahi due to poisoning," Maatre tells RK in dismay.

"What! Then how come both bodies are lying on the bed?"

"Sir, I took her body down. She was hanging half naked, and all the members of the society had gathered outside the house. So, to avoid embarrassment, I took her down," said Kushank, weeping.

"That's ok. I can understand, but why did you not cover them if you did so much?"

"Sorry, sir, we lost our mind when we took Divya down and could not decide what to do, seeing the two kids semi-naked. In the meantime, Lala ji asked us to not touch the bodies as per the police instructions. So we left them the way they were and followed the instructions."

"OK."

"Such fucking idiots, they can get the body down with bare hands without realizing that it will tamper evidence but cannot cover the same, which requires no touching," whispered RK to Maatre.

"Sir, please, let go. They are in a state of shock."

"I want all of you to examine, inch by inch, every corner of the room. Also, call Janhvi and her team."

Forensics also join soon, and both teams simultaneously examine the crime scene.

"Same case as Ziya," says Janhvi, looking at the bedroom lock.

"Meaning?" said RK with an enigmatic expression on his face.

"No forced entry. The room was locked from the inside, and no traces of a third party. Divya has died from choking a windpipe that is certainly due to hanging. While Mahi, due to poisoning."

"But why two modes of death? And if so, then the possibility of both dying together is very less because they are different modes of death," stated RK.

"What shit! What is wrong with the kids these days that is leading them to suicide? First, Ziya, and now these two. There is something not right. I can sense very well," continued RK, feeling the erroneous situation that was created.

"Well, RK, we will have to carry out a detailed examination in the hospital, and the evidence will speak for itself during the autopsy."

"Ok. Call the ambulance. Collect phones and send them to the lab immediately."

"Divya ate my son away. Bloody witch killed my son and took his life away," yelled Mrs. Joshi, pointing at Mrs. Salgaonkar.

"Mind your wagging tongue, or else you will be gone along with your son. My poor daughter ended her life because of Mahi. And you are accusing our little daughter," replied Mrs. Salgaonkar, agonized.

The two walked towards each other and started abusing, and it got worse when they went physical – slapping, pulling each other's hair, twisting arms.

"Nia, what are you looking at? Control the situation. Separate the two, or else we must arrest them." RK shouted at Nia, seeing that even she was the spectator of the ongoing nuisance.

"Yes, sir. Sorry, sir."

The two were separated after a lot of effort. RK walked towards the husbands and addressed them, "Look, Devendra ji and Kushank ji, I know you both, as parents, have lost your children, and it's very difficult to accept this reality. But you need to gather strength and take care of your better halves. I assure you that full justice will be served, and the truth will come out soon. I need to take Mahi and Divya's body for autopsy. The bodies will be returned as soon as the procedure is completed, and you can perform the last rites. Please, I request with folded hands to take charge of the situation."

Both the men nodded and assured full support to the authorities.

"C'mon, put the bodies in the ambulance, and let's take them to the hospital."

The unit left for further investigations.

The Next Day, 9 A.M.

RK is already at the hospital. "Dr. Chandra, this time, please come out with some positive results. I think Ziya and this case are interconnected. I don't want you to miss out on anything. We need to stop this," RK pleads with the doctor.

"Let us do our job, officer, and not jump to conclusions. There was nothing that we missed in the previous case. I am still very sure it was a clear case of suicide. And please don't teach me my job," replied Chandra harshly.

"Bloody swine of the highest order," murmured RK to himself.

"You said something?"

"Not at all. I just said, please continue."

In the room, the two bodies were lying next to each other on different beds.

"Let us start with Mahi first," Chandra ordered Janhvi.

"Okay, sir."

"Primarily, blue lips show the signs of poisoning. Nails also have turned blue. No struggle and no needle marks on the body. No signs of any force poisoning, which suggests the possibility of self-ingestion or knowingly accepting the poison through the oral cavity. Time of death between 12-1 p.m."

"Ok, sir."

"Let us dissect the stomach. Scalpel, please."

After cutting open the stomach wide, "Traces of poison found in the stomach confirm death due to intake. Send the traces for lab testing to Manjeet so we can know the exact nature of the poison."

"Sure, sir." Janhvi walks with the sample, hands it over to Manjeet, and asks him to send the results asap.

"Did you find anything?" RK stops Janhvi on the way to the autopsy room.

"In progress, but one thing for sure – Mahi died of poison intake. Now let me go, or else Chandra will kill me."

"What's new in this? We have known this since yesterday. Time pass," RK muttered again to himself.

"You took a lot of time to return, Janhvi. Did that psycho officer stop you?"

"No, sir, he was not seen. Actually, it took me time to find Manjeet."

"Hell, ok. Let us get to Divya now."

"Cause of death, asphyxia – blocking of the windpipe. No signs of any sexual abuse or any marks on the body. No struggle marks. So the cause of death by hanging is confirmed."

"Ok, sir."

"Scalpel, please."

Janhvi gives it to the doctor, and after cutting open the stomach, "So no signs of any poison or foreign particle. And the time of death is around 1-2 p.m.."

"So, sir, that means she hung herself after Mahi died? Then what was she doing in between, for whatever time she had?"

"Well, that leads me to conclude that she first killed Mahi. Subsequently, realizing the enormity of her mistake, she could not decide what to do and whom to reach out to for help. Finally, the fear of going to jail forced her to commit suicide."

"Sir, but why would she kill Mahi? Both of them were just 15."

"I don't know that. Maybe their phones would speak for them, but she killed Mahi. Also, not to forget before the autopsy, while undressing Divya's body, we found a bottle of poison hidden in her innerwear."

"Yes, sir, but I cannot take it that she killed."

"You take it or not, my report stands concluded with this. Also, does that idiot know about the bottle story? Did you hint or tell him anything?"

"NO, sir."

"I am sure you did not. Otherwise, that animal would not have kept quiet."

"Sir, please do not speak like this."

"Oh, miss has a soft corner. Let's go out, or else that animal will come in and pounce on us."

They exit the room, and the entire scenario is narrated to RK, including the hidden bottle. RK goes red after hearing about things being hidden from him but controls his anger. "Everything accepted but two things –

1. Why did Divya kill Mahi?
2. Divya was topless, and Mahi wore nothing at the bottom. Why were they lying semi-naked in this position? This hints at something, or is it just a baseless trace to divert our minds?"

"These are the two things that are worrying me. Well, let the cell phone records come. I think we shall be able to join the pieces of this unsolved puzzle," said RK.

Amid this, Manjeet comes running with the results, "Sir, the poison name is fipronil, mostly found in domestic cockroach killing sprays or others."

"Well then, it was easy for Divya to poison Mahi as it is easily available as an insecticide and needs no prescription," interrupted Janhvi.

"So RK, you have got the conclusion from my end, and this time, I have given you a killer, but the other still remains a suicide. And FYI, the two cases, Ziya's and this, are unrelated. Now goodbye and get out." With this, the doctor himself left very quickly to avoid any kind of drama.

"I want to kill this motherfucker, take him to the forest, and leave his body for vultures to conduct an autopsy."

"Let go, RK," Janhvi calmed him down.

The cell phone results were out by evening, and to everyone's surprise, nothing suspicious was found in the records, media, or any sort of data (like in the case of Ziya's suicide). The bodies were soon returned to the respective parents for last rites. The case was closed as both the accused and the victim were dead.

But RK was apprehensive about such deaths and was sure the two cases were connected. He was forced to shut the cases down due to a lack of evidence but continued to conduct a parallel investigation independently.

The New Year Tragedy

1ˢᵗ January, 11 A.M. at the Police Headquarters.

"Good morning, sir. Happy new year, sir," Maatre wished RK with a bright, excited smile.

"Maatre, we will find out soon about this new year. I am sure it won't be a happy one for us, but just for your sake – a happy new year to you, too. Get ready for the roller-coaster."

"Sir, you can be nice, at least on the first day of the year."

"Maatre darling, wait and watch. The killings are not going to stop. I am sure it's a trap, and soon we will hear about a new so-called suicide case."

"Sir, how can you be so confident?'"

"Well, there is something called as - gut feeling; you will know the same one fine day. I am hopeful and confident. But for that, you need to have some space and stop consuming extra calories. Look at your belly – if you wish to hug your wife, your belly will stop you from doing the same," teased RK and laughed out loud. Maatre felt embarrassed and helpless.

While the entire police station was enjoying the joke and laughing, the phone rang. As the phone continued to ring, Maatre's heartbeats rose, and he looked tense. He looked stunned at RK as he walked to pick up the landline. There was a sudden silence in the station, and the atmosphere turned stressed.

Somehow, Maatre picked up the phone and said in a frightened voice, "Hello. Who is this?'

"Give the phone to Ranbir Khandelwal," the person replied from the other end.

"May I know who is online? Ranbir sir is busy. You can tell me. I am senior constable Maatre."

"Maatre, I will suspend you. Just do as I say. This is CP Kishore Khaitan."

"Sorry, sir, Salaam sir. Sorry. RK sir had gone to the washroom and asked me to take charge. Sorry, sir, please forgive me. Here he comes. RK sir, CP sir for you online," shouted Maatre, even though RK was standing beside him and enjoying his antics.

"Sir, please don't tell anything to CP sir. I beg and promise to be your slave for the rest of my life," whispered Maatre to RK while handing the phone.

RK gave a cunning smile and gestured to Maatre to hold his ears and stand at one corner of the cabin until he finished his call. "Sir, Ranbir online."

"Ranbir, I want you to come to my office immediately."

"Sir, I will be there. *Jai hind*, sir." With this, RK cut the call.

"Constable Maatre. You are gone today. Sir has called me to his office. *Tu toh gaya*, Maatre (You are gone Maatre)."

"Sir, please, sir, save me, sir."

"Shut up and start the jeep. I will join in a minute."

"Sir."

As soon as they reach, RK says, "Maatre, you wait outside. I will go and see what it is about."

"Sir, you remember…"

"Shut up, Maatre, and wait for my orders," RK walks into the commissioner's cabin.

"Good morning, sir," RK greets the Commissioner of Police.

"Good morning, Ranbir. Please have a seat."

"Thank you, sir."

"Have a look at this file, Ranbir. I am just disgusted with whatever is happening in our state. This is not the way I wanted this year to start. But now that it has, just have a look at it."

Ranbir opens the file and cannot believe what he sees. Seven children celebrating new year's Eve die. "Sir, what the hell is this? Sorry for the language, but what is this?"

"Exactly! The same question the ministry is asking me. And has asked me to find a solution at the earliest, or we will see bad times very soon."

"Sir, that means?"

"Meaning *jaane de, mudde pe aa* Ranbir (Forget meaning, come to the point.) This was the first thing in the morning on my table, and all were just 17-year-old junior college kids. And read further, after the boy killed the other six, he then slit the nerve of his right wrist and died."

"Sir, also, did you notice this? The forensic report says that the psychotropic drug cocaine is found in the blood of these kids. That means these kids were either drugged or organized a rave party. Shit, man."

"What the hell! I missed out on this. Thanks, Ranbir. Now, without wasting any time, please get going."

"Sir, this is unbelievable. I have been shouting at the top of my voice that these cases are co-related, but I was silenced, and now, just because you are being pressured from the top, you want me to solve the mystery."

"Ranbir, stop complaining and start acting. I am giving you my full hand with no questions asked. That's not all. I am forming a unit – Child Special Task Force (CSTF), and putting you in charge. Also, to help you with this, you will jointly work with a central agency – Crime Against You (CAU). Akshay Kewadia and his CAU team are waiting at your police station."

"Sir, you should have heard my cries before, right after Ziya's case. Who knows, we could have saved these children."

"Ranbir, dismiss. Remember to choose a good team, utilize their capabilities, and get me results asap."

"Sir!" Ranbir left.

The Team and The Investigation

Ranbir addresses his team in the police station, "Guys, a new force – Child Special Task Force (CSTF) has been formed by the government to solve and stop these horrendous minor killings. I have been appointed as the head of this team and…"

Accolades are all around, and everybody congratulates him.

"Have you guys totally lost it? *Gaandu ki tarah taali maar rahe ho* (All of you are appreciating me like mad). I have not been promoted or awarded for something. I have been handed over the responsibility to save innocent children. Please understand the seriousness of the situation."

"Sorry, sir," comes an apology in sync from everybody.

"It's ok. So I am the head and will have in my team – Maatre, Shastri, and Nia from the police force. Janhvi will be helping us with the forensics and other technical stuff. Also, we have Akshay Kewadia and his team from the central body – Crime Against You (CAU), to help us throughout. AK sir over to you."

"Thanks, Ranbir. Ok, guys, we begin the investigation now but at a new office. Gather all the material, data, and whatever we have. Even the smallest detail should not be missed, and let's go to the new office location."

"Sir," comes in sync from the team. Everyone collects all data and evidence, whatever is on the case, and leaves for the new office at Madhi-Ghat.

As soon as they reach the location, everyone involved in the investigation looks awestricken, seeing the tech-savvy setup. The team is captivated and excited to work in the never-seen-before hi-tech office – the newly formed CSTF headquarters.

"Ok, guys, let's begin," addresses AK to the entire team, and immediately, each one settles into the allotted department and gets going.

"Let's see what we have on this," says RK, asking the team to highlight whatever they knew from the case. But everyone seemed confused and looked at each other blankly. The team, including RK, knew nothing new about the case in the past few weeks and stuck with the suicide theory.

"What! Why are you looking as if I have asked to donate your kidney or life or something? Stop giving that petrified look and give me something substantial. C'mon guys," continued RK, hoping someone would take the initiative and begin with the case files.

But there is absolute silence in the room. Nobody utters a word and just looks around.

"Shit, I can't believe my team. Everyone is behaving like dumbos. Forget it. Let's go one by one. Janhvi, give me the names and ages of the kids who lost their lives?"

"Ziya, Mahi, and Divya, all –15, the party group 17."

"That's it, copy that. We have the age group 15 to 17. Zero down on this and see if you guys can find something."

"Perfect, sir, on it." Janhvi gets going.

"Maatre, the death pattern in all three cases."

"Sir, Ziya hanged herself. Divya poisoned Mahi and killed herself again by hanging. The boy named Parin killed his friends by stabbing and then cut his wrist with the same knife."

"That shows suicide for sure. But the case where the others are killed before the accused kills himself shows that the so-called accused is forced to kill others before finishing himself. That means it is a planned murder."

"*Saahib*, how are you so sure about the accused being forced to murder?"

"Maatre, if that had not been the case, the accused would have either run away or surrendered but not ended his life. Also, these are young kids; without influence, they cannot commit such heinous crimes. Maatre, start finding a common link between these kids. Quick."

"Sir."

"I am scared this is not going to stop here. This is big, and it's going to consume a hell of a lot of kids," a worried AK shares his concern with RK.

"I totally agree with you, AK sir. Why don't you do one thing – ask your team to check with the technical angle. Go through all social media accounts, phone galleries, emails, and whatever is possible. We need to work in a reverse manner and rule out unimportant things rather than looking for clues."

"Good idea. Ranbir will be on it."

The Next Morning, 10 A.M.

"Sir, good morning. I have something for you. Please come with me," Janhvi takes RK to her workspace.

"C'mon Janhvi, high hopes. Please don't disappoint."

"Sure, sir, see this," Janhvi points at the computer screen.

"What! Are you sure?" says RK with apprehension.

"Dead sure, sir. All these kids aged 15 to 17 were about to appear for either the 10th or 12th standard board exams the same year. And that's not it…"

"Then?"

"These kids registered themselves online, and post-registration received admission cards through Doogle mail."

"Are you hinting and pointing towards…?"

"Exactly, sir. Doogle mail is the common source among these kids. Their appearance for the board exam is not as big a clue as much as Doogle is. But I'm stuck here. Is Doogle being used as a tool for crime, or is it a mere coincidence?"

"Well done, Janhvi, this is not a mere coincidence. Doogle is definitely involved, but 'how' is a new task. These are for sure tech-based crimes, and let me tell you, it will not be easy to fight."

"AK sir, we have got a lead," RK explains the entire scenario.

AK is taken by surprise. Rather, more of him is disappointed by RK and his team's claims, "Ranbir, are you serious? Are you asking me to work on this? How do we investigate Doogle? It is a US-based company, and we do not have any strong evidence. Even if we did, why would they allow us to enter their server without permission? And getting permission from the respective governments will take time. And surely, you know none of them will agree."

"But, Akshay sir…"

"Ranbir, don't be stupid and stop encouraging your team for things that look highly unrelatable to this case. Please stop wasting time. Dismiss."

Ranbir left dejected and went to his cabin.

"I am not letting this clue go. I am sure Doogle has something to do with this case," murmurs RK and calls Janhvi. "Janhvi, come to my cabin now."

"Janhvi, AK sir is not with us on this. We need to work on it separately and unofficially. Increase your force, channel your sources, and find a breakthrough before it's too late."

"Sure, sir."

CSTF was formed, and they carried on operations along with CAU. The suicidal killings were unstoppable; they continued to take place and slowly captured other parts of the country. This resulted in declaring CSTF a central body, and many branches of the investigating body were formed in different parts of the country. Sadly, even after 6 months and over 150 children losing their lives, they failed to find a breakthrough, except for the Doogle angle (Which stood not so substantial). The killings continued to jolt the country.

CHAPTER FIVE

The Entry of Guru-Cool

Uttarakhand, on the Streets of Badrinath

'Come, do Pooja, and I assure you your kids will be fine and their lives out of danger,' said a poster pasted on the wall (on the streets of Badrinath) of some holy man guaranteeing positive results after the rituals he performed. The poster just had a small picture of a man in white. It had no address or location, just one phone number with a name beside it – GURU JI.

The nation was in distress and had left people clueless. The parents were scared to leave their kids alone and go out, nor did they let them travel unassisted anywhere. No one knew the reason for these suicides, and as history has it, most believed this to be some kind of paranormal force hovering around.

Few saw posters and connected with Guru ji. They got the rituals done and felt positive after the same. The parents initially took a chance by leaving the kids alone for some time and experienced no adversities. Later, this confidence grew, and the kids were safe. The parents who took the Guru experience themselves became the advertisement source and did word-of-mouth publicity for the Guru ji.

Slowly and steadily, the Guru ji influence increased, and inversely proportional to this, the number of minor killings began to fall. It was difficult to understand whether this was the Guru effect or a mere coincidence, but his entry had benefited the country. The nation began to breathe in a more relaxed atmosphere, and things appeared to normalize.

Guruji's charm slowly captivated the entire nation. Reportedly, along with the minor killings, other cases like ghosts or evil spirits residing at flats, houses, and offices. All of those were wiped out gradually.

Guru ji believed there were no evil spirits. It's just the soul that seeks justice or, with an incomplete wish, persists on earth even after death. Guru ji could connect with these souls, fulfill their wishes, and help them attain salvation.

He slowly started giving lectures on humanity and brotherhood, too. Not believing in one religion or worshiping any particular God differentiated Guru from other Godmen. Even his appearance was unbiased and did not hint at any particular religion. He was dissimilar and looked as if here to stay forever to serve mankind.

The Press Conference

The Guru ji effect had spread all across the nation like fire. He did what the police officials, central agencies, government bodies, and all other investigating agencies could not. Yes, he could put a full stop to the minor killings. After losing more than 250 children across the country, the suicide pandemic (as it was called by everyone) came to a halt. Yes, you heard it right. Our very own Guru ji helped the nation overcome this adversity.

Also, Guru ji was different from other Godmen by not having an ashram of his own, not calling anyone in person, nor visiting or meeting anyone personally.

A press conference was held in a very unusual manner below the banyan tree, as the famous Guru ji denied a visit to any media office for the interview. After a short wait, Guru ji arrived as usual in his simplistic avatar in white clothes with no other accessories.

The media personnel were eager to shoot questions, and soon after taking his position, Guru ji gave the go-ahead, "Let's begin."

"Guru ji, this is Raj from Times World. My question is – you do not wear accessories representing any particular God, nor do you greet in any particular way. Can you please add some light on this topic? Also, don't forget you don't wear a beard or anything of that sort. I mean, you are a very atypical Guru ji. Why?"

"Hello, Raj. Nice to hear from you and happy to see you present. See, my ideology is simple – I am not restricted to any religion. I am not any God or Godman. I am God's messenger here because the Almighty has chosen me. We have always heard from the greats that GOD is ONE, then how can I be partial or biased toward any particular religion? If I greet or treat myself in a particular way, you guys will portray me as a restricted messenger. So you see, I am a Believer of ONE, follower of NONE."

The media personnel present were highly impressed by the ideology that Guru ji carried, and it was a never-before-heard reply for all, especially him saying GOD is ONE.

"Next, please," Guru ji asked to proceed with a smiling face.

"Guru ji, this is Sakina from The Country Magazine. Do you carry all your rituals in the open below a tree? Also, you do not have an ashram of your own. Isn't this very unlikely from the Saint or Guru culture we have seen over the years? Your take on this?"

Guru ji laughed aloud and replied, "I think you have problems seeing a smile on my face, or you do not like peace?"

"No. Nothing like that, Guru ji, it's just that we have never seen this kind of pattern in ages."

"Well, I don't wish to comment on that, but I believe in the most ancient philosophy of Gurukul – where disciples studied below the banyan tree in an open environment, and hence, I carry all my activities under a tree.

"Regarding your ashram question, we have seen many cases occurring in the ashrams off-late. I would not like to offend you all, but there have been a few instances where sexual abuse, drugs, human trafficking rackets, and other malpractices have been carried out. I have told you clearly that I wish to remain as a medium of God for the welfare of society. Nothing more, nothing less."

Everyone was stunned with such clear thoughts of this man. He was truly the man of his words.

"Guru ji, you don't have any name or anything. Why so? Sorry, I forgot to introduce myself. This is Razzaq from The Minar."

"See, you belong to a particular section of society, so you need a name to introduce yourself. For me, Humanity is the only religion. Adam and Eve did not have any religion; they were just humans, but today, if you had to classify them, you would consider them as Christians (as per the names hint), which may not even be true. So, my dear friend, name creates an image in our smart thinking system, and we as humans start categorizing people. So, it is good to be nameless rather than shameless," Guruji laughs aloud and ends the answer in his witty best.

Razzaq is amused by the reply and excitedly says, "Guruji, I have a name for you, and I am sure you will neither deny nor be disheartened. With your permission, if I may."

"Sure, go ahead. Let the thoughts flow, rather than letting them go."

"GURU-COOL. You are an ardent follower of the ancient philosophy and always cool with your answers, so, GURU-COOL."

"I love this, and you said it right. I appreciate your title of GURU-COOL."

And there are chants everywhere – "GURU-COOL, GURU-COOL, GURU-COOL."

"Hi Guruji, this is Mamta from the News NXT channel. My question is that all you said and did is fine, but why do you charge for the rituals or your good-doings."

"I was waiting for this one, Mamta. Thanks for asking me my favorite question. Everything comes with a price tag. The one that comes without any takes away something else of yours if not money. And this money is not for my personal use. I envision manufacturing medicines for all ailments, from fever to cancer, leaving none. And that too at never-before affordable pricing. This will serve my mission –the welfare of the society and make this world a better place to live."

"Guruji, there have been many before you that claimed the same thing but later became profitable companies and were listed on global indices. What is it that is going to be different in this case?" Mamta extended her question and looked forward to an answer.

"Mamta, it is a wait-and-watch game. You must see for yourself, as I believe in action, not acting (pretending).

Also, the main reason for this press conference today is the announcement of a new era in the field of medicine. We are starting seven pharmaceutical manufacturing plants in different parts of the country, the permission of which has already been passed by the Ministry of Health and is also USFDA approved."

With this, the media was taken aback as there were no leaks about the plan from Guruji, and the government, too, had kept it an utmost secret.

"Namaste Guru ji, this is Diler Khatri from Bharat TV. My question is, why just the medicinal field? Why not any other department? I mean, why so specific?"

"Rog mukt desh hi pragati ki raah pe chal sakta hai, kyun ki jaan hai toh jahaan hai. (A country free from ailments is always progressive; with good health, we can achieve whatever we wish). I want to be remembered as a Good Element of the society. That's it for today, thank you."

"Guruji, there are many other fields that need development that can revamp our country, like education, hospitals, and self-defense training for girls, to name a few. Why not these than just the pharma sector?" asked Diler distrustfully.

"Well, I stick to my words and would not like to comment if I don't have a rational response," Guruji left with that final answer. But there was something for the first time that made Guruji a little uncomfortable.

The nation was surprised by Guruji's announcement, which made headlines everywhere. He was called 'The GOOD ELEMENT, the GURU-COOL of the new era.' After a long time, something good had caught attention, and the killings had taken a backseat.

The Rise of One and Fall of Many

Guruji, as promised, inaugurated seven manufacturing units in different parts of the country, naming his company GUR-MED Pharmaceuticals Private Limited. Whatever money he got through rituals or as donations were directed to these units for producing medicines.

The units were well-planned, and every unit produced different medicines for different diseases. He continued living the way he did, and there were not any changes in his lifestyle. Truly, he was proving to be God's messenger sent for the welfare of society.

On the one hand, Guruji's GUR-MED pharma was capturing the market because of its equally efficient drug and very low pricing; on the other hand, competitive companies were slowly plunging and incurring losses. Slowly and steadily, the effect was also seen in the share market. Investors could foresee the big pharma giants losing hold of the market and began selling the stocks.

Due to overselling, many of the shares tanked like never before, and during this course, the ones who suffered the most were retail investors or, you may rightly say – the common man. It was a never-seen scenario in the history of the pharma industry, which affected the other sectors, too.

There were times in the past when a new company rose and captured the market for a short time, but the balance of the market remained unruffled. However, the rise of 'GUR-MED Pharmaceuticals Private Limited' was beyond normal. The situation soon turned out to be out of control to the extent the news of suicide (of the common man due to heavy losses he suffered in the share market) started to pour in from various parts of the country. The GUR-MED pharmaceutical's existence had become debatable. But the lower section of society was happy as they benefited like never before.

Again, on national demand, Guruji planned an open press conference. The stage was set, and it would be a fiery session. Guruji, as usual, arrived in his most simplistic avatar and took center stage. And he signaled the session open.

"Guruji, Aditya this side from NewsXpress. My question is, your company has taken the market by storm. What's your take on this?"

"Look, young man, I am not here to compete with anyone. I am just doing my job. Like you are working for your media company, I am working for God as His messenger and a well-wisher for the common man. I am not here to make profits, fill my pockets, and check my balance sheets. I am here so that mankind gets what it deserves without discrimination."

"But Guruji, your claim of benefiting the common man is taking the lives of others. How would you quote this as a fair move? This is Diler Khatri from Bharat TV. We had an encounter in your last press conference, too."

"Oh yes, I remember you very well. Look, dear, one who has come to this world has to leave someday. And the route of his departure is decided even before the birth. My full sympathies and condolences with the families of the deceased, but this is how it was meant to be for them," came a very typical answer.

"Guruji, now you are sounding like other ordinary baba's. Your charismatic way of answering seems missing, and the answers are unconvincing."

Guru-Cool looked like he was losing his cool, evident from his face, but somehow he maintained his calm. "Look, dear, what I meant was death is inevitable. And I believe in karma. Those ending their lives might have, at some point, trembled the balance of society and hence paid for it. *Niyati ka dastoor hai, tum chedhoge uss-se toh who tumhe nahi chhodega* (If you disturb the equilibrium of nature, nature will seek revenge on you.)."

"Sorry, Guruji, you were unimpressive then, and you are unimpressive now. How do I take such immature replies? Sorry."

"Next question, please," said Guruji, totally avoiding DK.

"Guruji, what is your next step? This plan shook the entire economy of the country. Now, what next? Is this it? Or something else is about to come? This is Jugal Nath from the Today News channel."

"The journey has just begun with the manufacturing units, and you will see retail outlets of our Ayurveda medicines. Our formulations will be way more potent and act faster than other brands available. We have come up with this plan to reduce the consumption of harmful drugs and treat severe disorders with the help of natural herbs available."

"This means Guruji, you not only plan to disrupt but aim to finish the market competition. The welfare factor appears nowhere in your talks nor in your deeds. My only concern is why and what are you up to?" an angry Diler Khatri interrupted.

"No comments," Guruji said and left. The intentions were made clear, but the motive was still hidden.

After a month, Guruji inaugurated his first store, Guru-Veda. His medicines were available in the market after two weeks and were an instant hit. After the first store's success (which was never a doubt), slowly and steadily, a chain of stores came up and was now present at 125 locations across the country.

The past few months were very petrifying for the economy of the country. Moreover, the government looked helpless as Guruji was not making money or letting anyone else do so. There were also requests from a few industrialists to implement a bill in the parliament for the minimum profit structure, but it seemed impossible.

As per the market analysts, this was the rise of the new low.

CHAPTER SIX

Aafat-E-Ulfat

Somewhere in the remote areas of Karachi, Pakistan, inside a bunker at the headquarters of Aafat-e-Ulfat…

"The world shall witness the never-seen-before destruction. The attack on India will make the souls of the entire humanity tremble. The entire chronicle will be remembered as the dark phase in the history of humanity," addressed Ishkar Ahmed, the chief of Aafat-e-Ulfat, to his army of more than 5,000 people.

"But, *Janaab*, it will be very important for us to execute the plan as decided and also not withdraw or step back under any circumstances," Akbar Ali, 1ˢᵗ lieutenant of the AEU, expressed his concern to Ishkar.

"Allah is with us. Because this time, it is not the regular battle of guns and goons. The outbreak will overshadow the fear of 9/11 in America or 26/11 in India. No red flags, hints, threat emails, or intimation. Just hit and let the world witness. It is what our poor enemy India would have never imagined, even in their nightmares."

"*Naara-e-Takbeer Allah-Hu-Akbar*," the entire troop vocalized with full gusto and adrenaline.

"Not to forget that we exist as torchbearers of Allah, and their aspiration of becoming a superpower will be set back by at least five decades. *Insha Allah! Naara-e-Takbeer*," roared Ishkar.

"*Allah-Hu-Akbar*," came a boisterous reply from the troop, outdoing the previous yell.

"Chief, but when are we going to attack? And when will the boys leave for India? We are all thrilled about the mission and looking forward to implementing it soon," said one from the crowd.

"*Kaafir bhai humaare taiyaar hai wahan Hindustan mei. Bhot zulm ka saamna kiya hai saalon se, ab intezaar mei hai humaare ishaare ke.* (Our brothers are already in India and waiting for my signal to attack. These local Indian Muslims have seen a lot in their lifetime, hence ready to seek revenge)."

The entire meet sounded very menacing and sent chills down the spine. If the blueprint seemed so dangerous, the execution should be outrageous.

After a Few Days

In a dimly lit room adorned with numerous screens, it provided a meticulously detailed, high-definition view of various locations across India. The server possessed direct access to distant CCTV cameras at these sites, rendering the imagery so vivid that no detail could escape notice. This strongly suggested that targets were already identified and the opportune moment awaited.

But more than 100 screens? Were they planning to hit all localities, or would few be spared? Or was there something that was hidden and not seen? This was not just big but a HUMONGOUS destructive planning.

"Apni aakhon ko gidd ki tarah screen pe jamaa lo, ek pal ke liye bhi nazron ko hatne mat dena. (Set your eyes on the screen and keep a constant watch without blinking)," addressed the Chief to his technical team.

"Just track every movement, observe every second, study every activity, and thoroughly note daily routine. I want no mistake. If there is any blunder, that person shall be chopped to pieces right in front of the entire assembly," Ishkar terrified his troop and instilled fear in them.

The course of keeping an eye continued. The same things were seen repeatedly and noted every day by the militants. Time passed by, and the wait appeared never-ending to the troop. They were raring to go, but no progress was hinted from the AEU Chief.

One Fine Day

"The team is doing good, *janaab*, and impatient to go. We have been checking every moment 24/7, and it's been over a month. I think it's time to take a call and give our enemy what it deserves the best," Akbar expresses to the Chief with excitement, a shrewd smile on his lips.

"Good is not enough, Akbar. We need to be the best. On previous occasions, our over-confidence has led to forceful giving away and pleading for mercy. This time, I want the operation to be full-proof."

"Ok, Chief, then let us wait and watch. I will also wait for your signal along with the boys," said Akbar in a low and sad tone.

Just when he was about to leave, Ishkar stopped him and said,

"*Murzaa mat mere yaar, Chhota sa nazraana hai taiyaar.* (Don't be upset, my friend; a small gift token is ready for you). Tomorrow, we take the first step toward our mission. Insha Allah, we shall succeed."

"*Janaab*, didn't get you. The first step means?"

"We have done the plotting and marking for the robbery. The CCTV of the areas that the boys are monitoring is our target. And our *kaafir* Muslim brothers in India will start working on it from tomorrow. This shall be our first step and an integral part of our operation. You will see it live with your own eyes in the same monitoring room."

"I am not aware of the robbery, but surely it sounds stimulating, and I'm waiting for the action to begin. *Naara-e-Takbeer.*"

"*Allah-hu-Akbar. Khuda Haafiz.* (Good Bye)," the Chief said and went to sleep.

CHAPTER SEVEN

The Mass Robbery in India

Morning 11 A.M.

A very ordinary morning, like any other day. Ishkar had set his monitoring at 111 locations in different parts of India. And interestingly, remote areas of the three-tier cities – cities that do not have great connectivity, are not very populated and are not as developed as metro cities like Mumbai and Delhi.

Somewhere in Pragatibaad

A person wearing a head-to-toe black suit, face covered with a black mask, enters a jewelry shop. He removes a gun from his pocket and keeps a bag on the table in front of the shop-keeper –

"Fill this bag with all the jewelry and cash available with you,'" warned the thief, pointing the gun toward the jewelry shop owner, Kailash.

"Sir, please, sir. Don't shoot, sir. I will give you whatever you ask for, but please don't press the trigger, please, sir," pleaded the owner with folded hands in a petrified tone. Kailash and his staff started pulling out all the gold jewelry on display and filling the bag.

"Quick! Also, ask your staff to get the cash and fill this bag simultaneously. And dare not try to reach out to the police or else…"

"Sir, please trust me. Nobody is involving the police. I am giving you all the jewelry available but cash! Cash, I don't have."

"Don't try to act smart. I know you do hawala (transfer of black money) business too. So without wasting my time, fill this bag with cash," he held the gun closer to Kailash and gestured to get the cash.

Kailash was stunned to hear about his hawala business from the conman's mouth. This forced him to think two things – either some competitor of his has tipped the conman about his secondary business (as he had many people against him and were jealous of his success), or the thief has been following all his activities for a long time.

Soon, the jewelry and cash were handed over to the conman, who left immediately on his bike.

"Hello, Pragatibaad police station. This is Kailash speaking from Mahalaxmi Jewelers. I have been looted, and everything has been taken. Please help. Please come, sir, quickly," Kailash informed the police as soon as the thief left.

Soon after the call, a team of three rushed to the spot. It took cops some time to reach, as the location was far and the connectivity was not great. Somehow, they reached after an hour of the loot, and the Senior Inspector Lalit Yadav said, "What happened here? Please do not miss out on the smallest of details and try to describe exactly as the incident occurred."

Kailash narrated the entire story in detail, frame by frame, to the officer and pleaded, "Sir, please help. He has taken away everything, from my earnings to my savings. Also, he has taken away the hawala cash, which wasn't mine and had to be given to my clients in the market. Sir, please help, or else I will have no option but to commit suicide."

"Already, you have done a crime by dealing in black money, and you want to commit another by attempting suicide. You dare not try! We will look into that matter later. First, show me this CCTV footage."

"SUZI, please show the last three hours recording," commanded Kailash.

"Sorry, I am having connectivity issues at the moment. Please try later after some time," came an unexpected reply from the STA.

"SUZI, show me recordings of the day," yelled Kailash at the device, forgetting it was inhuman and just a machine.

"Sorry."

"Shut up, SUZI, just shut up."

"Sir, what do I do?" a helpless Kailash asked SI Lalit.

"Well, in that case, Kailash ji, we will have to examine other CCTV cameras available in your surroundings and see if we can find something substantial. Until then, we are sorry, but we are totally helpless."

"Mishra ji (constable alongside Lalit), check with the CCTV cameras available in the nearby locations and see if you can get something out of it," ordered Lalit to his police aid.

"Sir."

After a minute, "Why are you still standing? Waiting for my birthday? Just leave and get me some clue before it gets dark and gray."

"Sorry, sir. You will have the evidence in a few hours. Jai Hind sir," Constable Mishra salutes SI Lalit and leaves immediately.

"Kailash ji, one last thing – can you give me an estimate of how much the thief has taken away from you? I mean the approximate value of jewelry and cash in total. If you can?"

"Sir ji, the exact figure is difficult, but around 80-90 lakhs in total."

"Are you kidding me? 90 lakhs! God bless you, Kailash ji, *Mahadev aapki raksha karein.* (May lord Shiva protect you)." The amount looted shook Lalit, and he, along with his team, left for the police station.

After some time in the police station at 4 P.M.

Constable Mishra arrives at the police station, hopeless and low.

"Mishra ji, you look miserable. I asked you to check the footage available near the shop and get something that could provide some breakthrough in the case and help us in further action. Almost after four hours of wait, you appear void of any confidence and seem low," Lalit said.

"Sir, you are right. The situation is not pleasing at all. There is barely any chance of clues that can help us proceed further. I gave my best shot but have been unable to crack down anything great."

"Mishra ji, stop annoying me and stop sounding like a loser. Update me on whatever you have, and let's get going."

"Sir, I have nothing with me. The CCTV cameras within 5 km of Mahalaxmi Jewelers are out of order and thus failed to record anything. I cross-checked with the local civic bodies, and to my shock, they told me the cameras had been inactive since last month. So you see, sir, we have absolutely nothing on this case."

"What the Fuck!"

"Exactly, sir. My reaction was the same. What the F! But to get at least some lead, I checked the cameras beyond 5 km but failed to find anything suspicious or clues. And sir, even before you doubt and double-check with the footage, let me tell you, I have already seen all the frames twice, and it is pointless to waste any more time on this matter."

Lalit looked lost and was aware of the tough times about to erupt in the case.

"Things don't look good at all. But also brings us to the conclusion that the conman is hiding nearby and within 5 km or maybe even closer. We must deploy a search party and try to nab that robber."

"But, sir, it will not be easy and will consume much time. Also, the sudden checking will create chaos if we start penetrating every corner of the city. This may lead to another possibility of the robber getting alert, which may increase the chances of him leaving the city," said another constable present at the police station.

"You are right, Bahadur, but we must take our chances. Bahadur, Mishra, and all of you at the station activate your informal sources and ask the entire network to monitor the market. The robber might try to sell gold jewelry in the market or spend way too much to buy needless stuff. Maybe. Tell your sources to report immediately if they suspect any activity or see anyone spending way beyond his capacity. And till then, let us begin the operation."

The Next Morning

A single loot in Pragatibaad and a theft of 90 lakhs were reported, which shook the entire village. But this was not the only con that occurred on that day. The next day, the news made headlines in the newspapers, and the media channels repeatedly flashed similar crimes in 110 other cities nationwide.

One hundred and eleven cities were looted with the same modus operandi on the same day across India. This hinted at mass robbery by a particular organization, which also meant further threats, as more than a hundred crores were siphoned off from the jewelry market (gold and cash jointly). The government bodies went pale and could not find the motive behind such a step.

The entire nation was in a state of shock and blamed the government for its incompetency. The whole jewelry market began to protest against the police force, and the visuals were absolutely horrifying. It was a never-seen-before or witnessed crime, and the result was outrageous. All the investigating bodies came into action with immediate effect. As per the Intelligence Bureau (IB), there were no red flags before the crime, and there were not any available even after, but coded something big was in the pipeline for sure.

The news captivated the entire nation in anger, and the print media and media channels were fueling the fire by covering these stories and repeatedly flashing the news 'Nation under Big Threat.' The government was under immense pressure, yet they hesitated to react due to the lack of clues. Unfortunately, they could also foresee a looming disaster – BIGGER and SCARIER.

The Breakthrough

The government faced enough criticism and went through many media trials. Also, the opposition was constantly doing rounds with blame games, and the pressure didn't look to ease anywhere soon. This annoyed the governing body and thus the Home Minister, MR. Adiraj Pandey decided to take matters into his hands.

Immediately, MR. Adiraj made a phone call to the CAU head, Akshay Kewadia.

"Akshay, Home Minister AP this side."

"Sir. Good morning, sir. Jai Hind."

"Akshay, there aren't any good mornings anymore. We cannot breathe in this atmosphere created by the media and the opposition. I am unable to answer the PM and sound idiotic every time I give him a new excuse whenever he asks me about the progress in the case," AP said with disgust.

"I absolutely get it, sir, and I'm on it day and night," replied AK in a depressed tone.

"The entire nation has its eyeballs fixed and hopes for some development. The topmost central investigating body is still figuring out things on this case, and like a statue in my cabin, I am awaiting the results or, for that matter, at least some kind of breakthrough. What do you expect? Me to get on the field and find a solution?" an angry Home Minister with no mood to accept any nonsense screwed AK.

"AP sir, we have some evidence but are waiting for it to authenticate. Also, sir, we are not to be blamed for this at all. We contacted police stations and those investigating the crime scene and found no clues due to local civic bodies' negligence. So, in short, it is the governmental bodies responsible for the delay and helplessness," an intimidated AK replied.

"Which means?"

"Sir, the cameras of those locations were non-functional and not only on the very day but since a month before that and are still out of order."

The firmness of his tone was digested, and the Home Minister said politely, "I will look into the matter personally and assure positive results in 24 hours, but I expect the same from you. Do whatever it takes, but give me closure on this or at least some lead."

"But, sir..."

The Home Minister disconnected the call without hearing the rest.

Disgusted, AK calls Ranbir to his cabin. "Ranbir, I want you to work with me on this countrywide robbery operation. Home Minister just called to screw my ass, and the mad man wants results in 24 hours."

"So? Why would I work to save your ass? Neither am I interested nor am I free."

"Ranbir, stop joking and being sarcastic. This is about national security. And I know we both are always on the same page when it comes to protecting the integrity of our country."

"You are right, AK, sir, but I know you don't like my working style and call me mad behind my back. Being called mad is still okay, as the entire world does, but stopping me from my work is not what I can take down easily."

"Ranbir, don't start all over again. We cannot question Doogle. Do you understand it is the world's most powerful company, residing in the world's most developed economy, the US?"

"Ok, I am ready to join you but need a free hand. No questions asked."

"Ranbir, you are asking too much and trying to misuse my helplessness. Well, okay, but remember you got to update me on every damn thing, even the smallest of the thing, without fail."

"Yes, sir." Ranbir left the cabin.

Ranbir returned and, from the door, said, "AK sir, why don't you join me outside and brief whatever we have until now on this robbery to the entire team? This will speed up the task and make life a little easier for all of us. Please, sir, if you may."

"Sure." They headed towards the core working space of the headquarters.

AK explained the events and gave them all he had gathered from the local police stations nationwide.

"Okay, guys, that's it! This is all I have; now you are on the same page. We need to nab these bastards at the earliest. Also, the intelligence agency and other investigating bodies have issued a red alert and tightened security. But we have nothing on anything. Absolutely nothing. Lastly, nobody is going home until we crack this."

"Thanks, AK sir, we are on it now. Come on, team, let's begin and try to arrange the scattered pieces of the puzzle. Let us see what we find by connecting these dots. Also, let us look at an angle of finding a connection between the two cases, if any," addressed Ranbir to his team.

"Ranbir, did I just hear connect? And which two cases?"

"Sir, the minor killings and this."

"Have you lost it?"

"Sir, you promised me something inside. And I believe you have a strong memory, so please let me be on it. I assure you the current case is the utmost priority for me and the entire team, but please do not interfere. Rather, it will be kind if you can help."

"Sure, please go ahead, but do not forget your promise, too. I will investigate from the other side with my team," Akshay said and left.

After a while, "Shastri ji, please get me the file of the first robbery at Pragatibaad."

Shastri came with the file, "Sir, but why only this file? The crime took place similarly at all locations, so why only this? Asked a clueless Shastri apprehensively while handing over the file.

"Because the first is always special. And there is surely something to emerge out of this case, is what I believe."

"Sir." Shastri left.

After a while, RK came to Janhvi's desk, "Janhvi, look at this and read it loudly," pointed RK from the file.

"The shop, Mahalaxmi Jewelers, was equipped with CCTV, and the application connected with a device named SUZI, but it had connectivity issues when examined. Sir, what does this mean?"

"Forget what it means. Can you do me a favor? Put the list of looted shops on your computer and search if device SUZI is found at these shops. Or if any other application, software, or anything is common in these. Explore the technical angle."

"On it, sir."

Janhvi starts screening the data, and to her surprise, "Sir, yes, found it. I am surprised that all these shops had SUZI in common, and all the devices were low due to connectivity or server issues."

"Well done, Janhvi. You may be amazed, but I am not. I was sure about the outcome, but I still wanted to double-check with my instinct. Did you find anything else in common? Any damn thing?"

"No, sir, just SUZI and the modus operandi are in common."

"That's it! Let's go to AK, sir."

RK and Janhvi proceed to AK's cabin. "Sir, may I come in?"

"Please come, Ranbir, have a seat. Janhvi, you as well. I knew you would provide us a breakthrough in this case, but this fast was not expected. Well done, my Karamchand 2.0."

"Janhvi, please go ahead," RK signals her.

"Ok. AK sir, we reviewed the entire file and all the info we had on this case. I entered the data into the system to look for similarities or co-relation. And to my surprise, one thing that has been highlighted is STA-SUZI."

"Who?" asked a bamboozled AK.

"Sir SUZI, the AI device. And it cannot be a coincidence that the server has weak or no signals simultaneously at different places across the country. The commonality shows a planned error, proving the server being hacked or bugged simultaneously to execute these robberies. And this is why we did not find any recordings."

"First, Doogle, now SUZI, what are you guys up to? I am unable to understand the way your team is working, Ranbir! We are here to find the evidence in the case, but it looks as if we are exploring the working method of these tech companies. C'mon Janhvi, you need to be more serious and not sound like Ranbir," an appalled AK scolded Janhvi.

And Janhvi went all silent after the rebuke.

"But AK sir, this is a big lead in this case. It cannot be a coincidence," continued RK with full faith in his findings.

"Ranbir! Ok, let me explain – Doogle is the world's leading software company; if not more, at least 3/4th of the world is dependent on this company's different applications for various reasons. Do I make sense?"

"Yes, sir, for sure you are right."

"Even your mail-id is with Doogle. The same is the case with SUZI. It is a part of every household and office, and its advanced versions are even used by big tech companies."

"I agree with you, AK sir, but we cannot deny the very fact – how this evidence has surfaced in this case. History has it – great technology has always accompanied greater crime possibilities. And in today's world, hacking any system is not at all difficult."

"Oh! So you are hinting that Doogle and SUZI have a bug in their respective systems and are unaware of it. If you are so damn confident, then why not try to intervene with their server. If you pass, we all proceed the way you want, but if you fail, you go nowhere but JAIL."

"I absolutely co-relate with what you say. Hence, I feel the United States is in this plan trying to plant something big against us."

"FUCK, Ranbir. Just get out. I am not going to report this crappy shit to the Home Minister. He will suspend me for sure. Go find something considerable and let me also work. Just get up and get lost."

Ranbir and Janhvi left the cabin but were not ready to let go of the SUZI factor. They were clear in their heads and knew which direction to follow.

The entire team kept investigating, and late at night, at 1 a.m.

"Yes, this is a major breakthrough, and I am sure even AK sir would agree," murmured RK excitedly. RK got up and walked towards AK sir's cabin.

"Sir, may I come in?"

"C'mon Ranbir, not again. You better come in at your own risk. If you sound stupid this time, I will expel you from all the cases and make sure you get suspended. Please come in," AK replied in a disgusted tone.

"Thanks for not believing in me, but it doesn't matter. I am here to show you something."

RK placed his laptop right in front of AK and showed him the CCTV footage of the crime scenes. "What is this, Ranbir? You show me two months of backdated footage, even before the crime occurred. What am I supposed to look for?"

"Sir, notice carefully and try to find the previously missed hints."

"Ranbir, I give up. Please tell me what is it?"

"Okay, sir. So one by one, open the snapshots I have taken and stored in a folder named 'Imp' on the home screen, and you will see the connection yourself."

AK opens the folder, checks all the images, and to his surprise, he finds Guru-Veda (retail Ayurveda stores of Guru ji) stores at every location where the crime occurred. And that's not it. These stores shared a common wall with the jewelry shop at all the crime scenes.

"What the hell is this? This Guru-Veda store is at every crime scene and appears as if target marking is done for the plan."

"BINGO! Now you get this. The targets were locked, and the stores were the sign."

"So the crime occurred at all the places where these Guru stores were present?"

"So, sir, here is a small catch. There are 125 stores of Guru-Veda, but the crime occurred at 111 locations. I suspect they did not plan an attack at all 125 locations, just to rule out the obviousness and avoid any noticeable attention."

"Well, Ranbir, I agree with you on this. This is serious, but my only doubt is –

Why would Guru ji do anything like this? I mean, how would he benefit from all this?"

"Sir, he is no Guru and nor any messenger of God. He has just played with the emotions of the country. He came from nowhere, and the minor killings stopped. How that's even possible is still a question mark to me. His entire setup of pharma units was a move to divert minds. Full marks to him for planning this well and executing these crimes perfectly."

"What do we do next, Ranbir? We need to find some strong evidence before arresting Guru ji."

"I know, sir. And this is what is worrying me. I am clueless this time."

"C'mon Ranbir, you cannot do that. You are the only person I know who doesn't give up on all odds and finds something even out of nothing. Think. I am sure you will figure out something. C'mon Ranbir, we have a lead and can't let this go away."

Ranbir thinks for a while. He takes his phone from his pocket and dials a number, "Hello, am I speaking to Diler Khatri?"

"Who the hell are you? Bloody fucker do you know what time it is? It is 3 a.m. Yes, this is Diler on this side. And I will fuck your ass, you asshole. Tell me, who is on the other side?"

"Sorry to disturb you, Diler, at this hour of the night. But it was urgent; otherwise, I would not have disturbed you."

"*Bhenchod paheli bujhaana bandh kar, bol kaun raha hai? Bhenchod naam aur kaam bataa warna meri lath aur teri gaand, dekh lena.* (Motherfucker, who the hell is talking, and what do you want? Better speak, or else I will turn your ass red)," Diler continued the abuse non-stop.

"Oh, sorry! This is Ranbir Khandelwal, speaking from CSTF. I wanted to talk to you regarding Guru ji. I am looking for help in a case, and I am sure you can support us."

"RK, sir! Sorry sir. I am extremely sorry," came a guilty apology. Diler immediately changed his attitude and way of speaking.

"It is alright. Diler, I want you to carry a background check on this Guru ji and find out things like – his origin, where he came from, his life before this, his family, and gather all sorts of information whatever is available."

"Sir, sure. I am not in favor of this Guru ji from the very first day and believe he is fake. But, sir, I will need your help to reach out to a few places. Also, you need to ensure my family's safety in my absence. Just one doubt, sir- WHY ME?"

"Diler, rest assured about the security, and yes, of course, there will be two officers from my team with you all the time. And why you? Because I have followed you since the time you entered journalism. You go beyond boundaries to find out the truth and have also exposed a lot of scams. And this one is about a national threat. Who better than you?"

"Thanks, sir, and I will be on it. When do we start?"

"Tomorrow morning at my office at 10 a.m." He disconnects.

"Are you sure, Ranbir, this will help? You don't trust our officers? Don't you think they are more trained, able, and equipped for this? I mean, I see no point involving a third party," questioned AK, doubting Ranbir's move on choosing an unverified media person over the entire capable force.

"Sir, trust me. He will neither upset you nor prove me wrong. He will hold true to his name and give the desired results at any cost."

"Ok then, my full co-operation on this, let's get going."

The next day, at 10 a.m. sharp, DK reaches the CSTF office and walks towards Ranbir's cabin, "Sir, may I come in?"

"Yes, DK, please do. Tell me, do you have a plan? One minute, please."

RK picked up the phone and connected to AK, "Sir, could you please come to my cabin? Diler is here."

AK joins them in the discussion.

"Sir, you are the same as me, to the point. We are going to have a good time together. Coming to the plan, sir, I want you to create different avatars of this Guru ji and give me."

"Avatars? Sorry, I didn't get you?"

"Sir, surely this Guru ji is not himself and was not born religion-free. He talks about his sudden appearance, but someone must have got him into this world, right? It is impossible that he walked out of the smoke, rose from beneath the earth, or came from clouds and chose only our country for this welfare stuff. There got to be some history of his."

"Absolutely, DK. I agree with you and understand what you say. But what kind of avatars are you looking for exactly? If you could please elaborate."

"Certainly, sir. I want you to create his avatars with a mustache, different beard styles, and various hairstyles. Reverse aging (using AI) to check how he used to look in his younger days and all that. I mean everything we can do to ease this case a bit."

"Good idea," interrupts AK. "Ranbir, I must say, your bet on this guy already seems successful and makes me feel more confident. Good going, young man."

"Thank you, sir. So once we have different avatars of this Guru, we can proceed by circulating the photographs within my sources and wait for sure shot results."

"I like your confidence, DK. We are on it right away." AK rushed out of the cabin immediately.

Ranbir got off the chair, and as soon as he was about to leave his cabin – "Ranbir sir, one minute," interrupted DK.

"Yes."

"Sir, you RK, me DK, and the one who left was AK. What a coincidence. Once we finish the case and taste success, we will be called the 'KKK.' Just imagine, like Rajamouli sir's RRR, we will be KKK."

Ranbir, with a disgusted expression, "Are you done? Shall we proceed with the case? Or should I say ACTION?"

"Sorry, sir, I just got carried away. Please, after you."

The entire situation was explained to Janhvi. She and her team went on to create different looks, leaving everything else aside. After much effort and permutations, they came up with fifteen combinations. They took out the prints and handed them over to DK.

"Well, DK, now everything relies on you. Surely, we, too, will circulate these photographs and look out for leads, but we trust your network more. Go ahead, and wish you the best. And these officers – Kamal Nath and Alok Tripathi – will be with you 24/7," a hopeful RK wished DK and prayed for success. Ranbir knew this was the beginning, and soon, the mystery would unfold layer by layer.

"Thanks, sir." DK left the office with the officers.

Soon, DK made copies of the photographs and circulated them.

At the Same Time, in Pakistan, at the Aafat-e-Ulfat Bunker

"Subhan Allah, mission ki mooh dikhaai par aap sab ko bhot bhot Mubarak. Hum pehla padhaav paar kar chuke hai. (Congratulations to all; we have successfully accomplished the first step). Insha Allah, we shall succeed in the rest of the mission too," the Chief addressed the troop in the assembly hall with a huge smile.

"*Janaab*, you have given us a reason to revel, and our chests swell with pride and happiness. We promise to do whatever it takes to accomplish victory in the mission," replied Akbar out of full enthusiasm.

"You all have to be mere spectators this time. The robbed money has reached the sources, and they will take care of the mission. Just buckle up, hold your seats tight, and see the action unfold like a thriller step by step by step. Ha ha ha…"

"*Janaab*, your monstrous laugh indicates the intensity of the action; we all pray the mission goes as per plan."

And Ishkar leaves the hall.

CHAPTER EIGHT

The Death Pool

The D-Day, 10 A.M.

A wonderful Sunday morning at one of the largest water parks in the world – Splash 'N' Wet water park. A luxurious water park spread over 15 acres of land, an entertaining treat for the family. The rain God added more fun to the day as it poured heavily, and by the look of the dark clouds, the rain appeared in no mood to stop. Everyone looked forward to enjoying the adventurous water park, complemented by the great weather. There were smiles everywhere.

At the entrance of the water park, there is this lucky mascot of Splash 'N' Wet, in the cute PENGUIN avatar, giving high-fives to everyone entering. He is teasing the little ones by showing candies and not giving them easily. As soon as the tiny ones reach his hand, he raises it even higher, to a distance beyond their reach. But in the end, give them candy and a big reason to be happy. Also, he is distributing balloons to the ladies and mascot merchandize and wristbands to men. Well, there was something for everyone that made them excited.

Inside the Water Park

To the extreme right, kids love the mini water park, full of enticing rides. The sprinkling artificial shower with water pouring down at a force, beating the natural force of the rains, has become the center of attraction for all the kids present. Some kids are slipping from rides, some splashing water on each other, some playing different games with the ball, some just floating in their cute different shape tubes, and the rest seem to sit in the pool and just enjoy the water flow.

To the extreme left is the huge wave pool spread across an acre. Just next to the wave pool is a huge yacht where DJ has his setup. He is playing the irresistible foot-tapping Bollywood numbers. People in the wave pool are trying to shake their booty and dance but can barely withstand the force with which waves are hitting them. People are laughing, cackling, hooting, humming the songs played at the top of their voices, and trying to dance. Just happy vibes and joyful energies all around.

At the center of the park is an enclosed toddler play area consisting of swings, slides, a mini trampoline, and walls painted with cartoon characters. Caretakers are looking after the toddlers, ensuring there are no mishaps. Activities like drawing, crafts, and drama are also carried out to engage the little ones. Most parents have left their children in this section to enjoy the water park. The toddlers also seem to have forgotten their parents and having an amazing time in this super electrifying and jolly atmosphere.

Water rides are spread at the different parts of the water park, well distanced from each other to avoid mixing queues. Hundreds await their turn in the queue at every adventure slide. Few rides are gigantic and look sky-high, almost 500 feet above ground level. The rides looked scary but amusing at the same time. The one experiencing the ride at his/her turn screamed his lungs out, outdoing his fear.

Finally, there are different cuisine restaurants next to the toddler play area, where everyone looks to relish the food of their choice. Apart from this, various small stand-alone stalls across the property have games like shooting, archery, mini-gambling, and darts. There are also stalls selling eateries like candies, snacks, etc. And there were selfie points all around, the must be anywhere and everywhere to capture the mesmerizing moments of this water adventure.

Suddenly, there is an announcement from the ticketing counter – "Guys, we have crossed the highest number of entries ever and recorded 7000 until now and still counting. On this happy occasion, the management has decided to provide a flat 15% discount on the purchase of all food items and merchandize. Enjoy. Cheers."

"Cheers," the crowd roars excitedly, and their happiness is boundless. It was like the icing on the cake for everyone present.

After an hour or so, suddenly –

"Help, help," come cries from many in the wave pool as the waves appear to come with increased force and heaviness.

For some time, the others in the pool can help, but soon, even they lose control. While the management checks the security, the lifeguards jump into the pool to help those drowning. But the pressure just doesn't seem to reduce, and the situation soon turns chaotic.

In the control room-

"Sir, we cannot control the wave pressure, and even the hydrofoil controller is not working. The situation is really bad, and hundreds of people are stuck at the deep end of the wave pool," says the management team to the water park supervisor.

"This isn't good news. I checked this personally. Those at the end cannot breathe or hold their breaths for long. Also, lifeguards cannot reach the extreme side of the wave pool, as they need to swim against the force. We must find a solution soon, or we will witness what we never thought."

As soon as the supervisor and his team leave the control room, they see a stampede. The situation turns frenzy. People just run in the exit direction without stopping. Somehow, the supervisor manages to stop one of the visitors and asks, "What happened, mam?"

"Dead bodies are floating in the wave pool."

"What?" The management says with shock, and they run towards the wave pool.

As soon as they reach the pool, their eyes widen in disbelief. The pool looks like a death pool. They see the alarming waves throwing bodies with full force toward the shore while a few lightweight bodies oscillate to and fro along with the waves.

"Sir, what do we do now? We need to stop this somehow," Manager Rahul cries, looking at the frightening sight.

Meanwhile, the supervisor shouts, "Shahsikant, stop," when one of his personnel heads towards the pool to check for the error.

As soon as Shashikant touches the water, he trembles as if shock passes through his body and dies in seconds. The episode that the management team witnessed blew their minds away. They look stunned, numb, and immovable for minutes after the electrocution.

"Sir, let's save the kids in the mini-pool. Run, sir, fast," says one from the management team. Soon, the team gathers strength and runs toward the mini-pool. The situation seems no different there. The entire pool looked like a cemetery, with kids' bodies afloat everywhere.

After more than two hours of horror and nightmare, the waves stopped automatically, and the running water in the kid's pool, rides, slide, and everything else stopped. The view was absolutely horrifying. There were bodies all around, not only in the two pools but also due to stampede and water slides. Few jumped from the waiting areas of the rides from that height and lost their lives.

The water park had turned into a graveyard. There were abundant casualties. The death toll was unknown but not less than half the people who visited. None knew that something like this could happen at a water park.

Soon, the doctors, ambulance, firemen, and police force reached the venue. Even the army followed. All those who arrived and, fortunately alive, were traumatized by what they witnessed. First and foremost, everyone headed towards helping the injured and ensuring they got the correct treatment. Those seriously wounded were transported to nearby hospitals, and those with minor bruises were treated on the spot. It took hours to rescue the alive, and it was late evening by then.

Finally, it was time to separate the dead from the pool. But the question was where to take them and how to deal with them. The bodies turned extremely heavy as the water got into them. It was impossible to transport them to their respective destinations.

Everyone seemed clueless when one army officer said, "I was with my battalion on a mission. We were around 200 soldiers and were heading towards an enemy bunker. To our surprise, there was not one, but ten bunkers. Not only did our information prove to be incorrect, but also we were 200 v/s 500-600 enemies. We still fought with great valor and did a lot of damage, but we had to withdraw due to a lack of force and losing more than 150 soldiers. The backup was sent, but it took them 24 hours to reach. We again attacked and, this time won the battle. But could not get the deceased fellow brothers who lost lives during the battle back in India, as they were already mass cremated and only ashes were left."

"Sir, with all due respect, how can we just cremate everyone? We know there are people of various religions amongst the dead, and we cannot hurt their sentiments," replied the park manager, Rahul.

"So, sir, what do we do? If we go as per your say, we will have to check the identities of every individual lying out there, distinguish them, and then decide to cremate or bury them. Right? And this endless procedure would take more than a week. What do you have to say?"

Hearing this, the manager kept mum. "Let me check with the higher authorities, and we will go as per the orders," came a reply from Assistant Commissioner of Police Mr. Jacob Abraham, present at the park.

ACP called the chief minister's office and explained the situation. "Let us go by what the army officer suggested. We have got orders directly from the CM himself. Just remember one thing: if anyone asks about this step – just say it was the most favorable one per the circumstances. Nobody differs from this answer and speaks no less or more. Is that clear, everyone?" asked the ACP sternly to everyone present.

"Yes, sir," came the reply in sync.

"But where do we cremate? We need an open ground for the same. If we do it in an enclosed area, there are further chances of other things catching fire," said Rahul.

"In the parking lot. There is ample space," prompted the supervisor.

The operation began, and transferring these bodies from wherever they lay to the parking area was not easy. There were a few who were assigned to take out their car from the parking lot and park in the vacant places inside the water park or outside on the road. The bodies were transferred with the help of cranes, helicopters, ambulances, and big lorries. This went on for almost 12 hours non-stop. A few bodies began to deteriorate during the course, but no one stopped. Finally, the mass cremation happened.

In the bunker at the headquarters of Aafat-e-Ulfat –

The tragedy was seen like a live telecast by Ishkar Ahmed and his troop. They celebrated the human loss, which was absolutely inhuman. The guys didn't even blink once during the entire operation. And there were chantings all around continuously of *'Naara-e-Takbeer. Allah-Hu-Akbar.'*

72 hours after the tragedy, at a press conference in India –

"Jacob, sir, what we experienced three days back was tragic and beyond a nightmare. Your take on this?"

"Look, we are investigating the matter and are equally moved by what happened. You guys just heard stories and questions thrown at us. We have witnessed all and still get jitters even at the thought. I would request you all to not make this a TRP topic."

"Sir, but how did it happen?"

"Well, it appeared like a technical error to us but still investigating if anything else. We have all the concerned teams, like forensics, technical experts, and others, on board to rule out doubts. We should be out with results soon and address the matter again."

"Sir, what about the mass cremation? Do you think it was the right call to take?"

"Well, it was the best decision taken by the look of the situation. I don't think it was possible to deal with it in any other way."

"Sir…"

ACP stopped the media personnel in mid-question and said, "That's all for now. We will update you with any new findings in the case. Thank you." The press conference ended there.

The entire nation was mourning the incident. The good thing was that there were no live clips or photographs of the incident that saved the nation from depression. The past few months had been disturbing for the country.

After two weeks came the reports stating the reason behind the tragedy was the technical failure, and the case was shut down by the local police.

CHAPTER NINE

The Unmasking

The nation was petrified and had never thought such a catastrophe could happen. Waves of grief spread across the country. Thousands lost their lives, and their families were inconsolable that they could not bid goodbye to their loved ones. Out of hundreds of casualties, a few lost their lives. Many were extremely critical, and many were badly injured.

In the midst of all this came a piece of news from Diler –

"Hello, RK sir, DK here."

"Yes, DK, tell me. Any leads? Please tell me that you have some news on that bastard."

"Sir, this Guru has been identified by a source in Islamabad, Pakistan. He is sending me the file, and I shall receive it by tomorrow afternoon at the earliest. I will meet you immediately after I receive the proof."

"WHAT! Islamabad, Pakistan? Are you sure?"

"Yes, sir. It's not safe to be on call for so long. Already, I have made a lot of enemies in the process of finding the truth. See you tomorrow, and hopefully, this shall it be." DK disconnected the call.

"Sir, we have identified the Guru and shall have everything about him by tomorrow evening. DK has done it, sir. But he sounded like he was being watched and followed," Ranbir shared the news with AK.

"Good. Now, it's just a matter of time. Let's wait for the evidence. Also, coming to DK, we would tighten up his security once he gets in touch. Till then, ask more officers to be around his house and ask them to take position immediately."

The team waited with all optimism. In almost 24 hours, the team highlighted all the occurrences that could help them in the closure. The team was confident that they were close to solving the case, and the environment in the CSTF had just eased a little bit.

The Next Evening, 7 P.M.

DK comes to the CSTF office with the file. As soon as he walks in, everyone applauds his bravery. Everyone congratulated him for whatever he did without being an official part of the investigating team. Few even saluted him for his courage and valor.

"Thank you all. Now, let's get to work. We have a long way to go, and the path is not easy," DK addressed everyone.

"DK, what do we have? We cannot wait any more," an impatient RK approached DK.

AK soon joined the conversation when informed about DK's arrival.

"Well, the news is not good. Guru is the former chief of Aafat-e-Ulfat, a Pakistani terrorist organization whose true name is Sayyed-Ul-Haq. This file has everything about him," DK handed over the file to RK.

RK and AK both very carefully looked at the file. They studied the information thoroughly, which had his old photographs, but the current photo of Guru ji looked a bit different than the old ones. It seemed like a fifty percent match.

They also studied the events that occurred in his life since childhood – from being a scholar during school days to a great engineer in those times to getting influenced by the ideologies that made India his biggest enemy. It was all there. But it also had his death certificate, and the proof spoke of him being finished in the famous plane crash in China five years ago.

"Thanks, DK. This looks a bit complex and needs a deeper study. We highly appreciate the courage with which you have helped us on this case. You may leave for now, but we will contact you if there is anything. Thanks a ton again. We all owe you a big time," AK acknowledged and asked Diler to leave.

"Welcome, sir," DK said and began to walk out of the office.

"And yes, the security continues to be around you and your family until the case gets solved. So need not worry," said AK.

DK left with a huge smile and a sense of pride.

The unit was behind the case and ready to unveil the mystery. Everyone pledged to work non-stop until the results were out. As time passed, things got clear, and the facts were right before their eyes. After a week, the two major findings in the case which held utmost importance were –

1. A planned air crash
2. Sayyed underwent plastic surgery to change his look. The team reached the doctor who performed the surgery on Sayyed, and he verified the same.

"It's time to get ready and nab the fucker," an infuriated AK told Ranbir.

"But AK sir, if we do it officially, we may have a tough time. The followers of Guru may not even allow his arrest and can attack us. On the flip side, if we reveal his identity, it will create chaos across the country, and we might not be able to reach the main reason or culprit," replied Ranbir with full concern.

"The situation is alarming, and we need to act at the earliest," continued RK.

"Then let us do it unofficially," replied AK. RK was stunned by this reply from AK sir, as it was least expected from him.

"But sir. What about the protocol?" questioned RK.

"C'mon, don't try to double-check RK. It's a go-ahead from my side, and I take full responsibility for the consequences.

Come what may, we will not leave this asshole. It's time to take the real element out of the fake Guru. Go get him. This project will be called – FOX HUNT."

The team was divided into two units. They started working simultaneously on the project 'Fox Hunt.' On the one hand, the team in the office was coordinating with Indian agents in Pakistan for Sayyed's weak link (if any) in full swing. On the other hand, the field team was studying the regular routine of Guru and keeping an eye on his daily activities.

The task was not easy, and the unit was running out of time, but still, the team was determined to the success of 'Fox Hunt.'

Finally, after a week, the agents in Pakistan got a breakthrough and could identify Sayyed's family. The complete family was under close surveillance and was tracked 24/7. Now, the total focus shifted towards catching Guru, and it was just a matter of time.

After a long wait, they finally successfully kidnapped Sayyed alias Guru ji. He was taken to a safe house far from the city area, in the forests, and ensured no civilians were around. As soon as they reached the safe house, Guru was unmasked.

AK and his team took Sayyed to a room, seated him on a chair, and tied him tightly with the rope. The room had various pictures of the terrorist organization Aafat-e-Ulfat pasted on the wall. The pictures depicted the entire road map of Aafat-e-Ulfat, from its formation to its recent activities, including minor killings, robbery, and the water park tragedy. It looked scary and quivered with the nature of operations carried out by the organization, but it was a bitter truth and undeniable.

As soon as AK and his team were ready to proceed with interrogation, they removed the blindfold. When Sayyed opened his eyes, it was like a shocker to him to see whatever was around, and somehow, he sensed something really bad coming his way (which was soon going to turn true).

"What the hell is this? What do you all want? Is this some kind of a joke?" Guruji asked furiously to everyone in the room, struggling to get away with the rope and trying to untangle himself.

"No hello, no Namaste, no greetings, directly what the hell? This is not how we know you, Guru ji. You are God's messenger, and you must help the one in need. We are your ardent followers and die-hard fans. Please help us," said AK with a wicked smile, getting closer to Guru ji.

His every step closer instilled fear in Sayyed, and he began sweating in the air-conditioned room. This was the first sign of him being related to the case. Everyone was all smiles in the room. AK came next to Sayyed's chair.

"Fans, followers? What kind of fans? Rubbish. And you, whoever you are, please stay away and talk from afar. Whatever the problem be, tell me, and I shall solve the same. But from far and not so close," Guru almost pleaded, shivering.

"Guru ji, why are you shivering? We are not here to cause you harm or something. We will just ask you riddles, and you have to solve them. If you give a wrong answer, you will be punished by this rude and impolite officer," warned AK, pointing towards Ranbir.

"By the way, Ranbir, why don't you introduce yourself? I am sure it will be an honor for him to meet you. Please go ahead, I mean literally, walk ahead towards him," AK hinted to Ranbir to continue and take charge of the interrogation.

Ranbir walked in full impudence towards Guru, infuriated, and his expression clearly showed that he was in no mood to take any nonsense.

Ranbir banged the table angrily, "Look, we know you are no Guru. You better start speaking the truth non-stop. We have already lost all our patience and energy in this case, and especially, it's very difficult for me to control myself," said Ranbir, looking in the eyes of Guru.

"What truth? The reality is right in front of you. Every bit of me, right in front of you, is genuine, and I am not hiding anything. I think you guys need help, especially you, my boy (pointing towards RK), and I am here for the same. Please share your suffering, and I shall be able to free you from all that is bothering you," calmingly, Guru ji addressed Ranbir's anger and asked him to be composed.

Ranbir turned towards AK, frustrated. "AK sir, this nonsense will not stop. He will not speak until we scare him. Rather, show him on the video call. Let us cut the crap and get to work immediately. Not to forget he is a trained militant."

"What scare and show what? Who told you I am a militant? I am God's messenger and…" replied the Guru, losing his calmness.

"Shut the fuck up. Who the hell is this," RK placed Sayyed's old pic before him and asked him furiously.

Sayyed gave a gesture of denial.

"This is you, swine. You have been trying to hurt our countrymen, and we, like fools, have been worshiping you. Everybody got trapped and forgot that no God messenger is possible today, and nobody serves humanity. People believed in you. We know you are a militant, but at least at some point, you should have thought before doing what you did," shouted RK emotionally.

"I think Ranbir, it's time to surprise him with our gift for him," intervened AK.

"Janhvi, connect me to Kabir Dewan at Bahawalpur, Pakistan," ordered AK to Janhvi.

As soon as Guru heard the name of Bahawalpur, his eyes popped out, and he started to lose his strut. It seemed he wanted to tell something, but CSTF was in no mood to stop.

"Sir connected, and Kabir is on call, live. I am patching to the big screen, just a moment," and all, including Guru, saw the video on the screen.

On the video call, AK to Kabir, "Hi Kabir, are we all set for the mission?"

"Yes, sir," and with this, Kabir flaunted the inner side of the jacket. He had a dozen hand grenades hung and two Glock pistols with 16 rounds of fire each.

"What the hell is this? What are you guys up to? And why is your officer at Bahawalpur?" questioned Guru with his mellowed tone.

"You will soon see for yourself and experience the action extravaganza," added AK, asking Kabir to proceed to the house seen behind him in the video.

Kabir went ahead towards the door and knocked on it twice. Nobody opened. He knocked again, and an old lady opened the gate this time. She looked confused and could not recognize Kabir.

"*Salaam, bibi-jaan,*" Kabir greeted the old lady.

"*Wa-Alaikum-Salaam!* Sorry, but I don't recognize you," replied the old lady.

"I am Kabir, Ashfaq's friend. Had come home with him last Friday for dinner. You forgot, *bibi?*"

"Oh yes! It slipped my mind. I have turned old, so I find it difficult to recognize or remember anyone except my family."

"I understand, and it is absolutely fine. Is Ashfaq at home?"

"Ashfaq has gone to the market for some work. He shall be back in an hour. You come in. Please sit and have some *kaava* or tea."

"No, *bibi*, I will come back later," Kabir started walking. He had just covered 100 odd meters when a huge SUV halted outside the old lady's house. The door opened, ten children exited the car with a lady, and they walked inside the old lady's house.

Looking at the episode unfolding, Guru ji pleaded, "What do you guys want? Tell me what you want? I will tell you everything I know. Just don't harm my family. Please, I beg you," he was down on his knees along with the chair in no time.

"Kabir, hold the mission for now and wait for my signal," AK ordered, disconnecting the video call.

"Start with your introduction, and don't stop. Do what you are best at. Just blabber all the shit non-stop. If we feel you are trying to be smart, then you have seen the trailer for yourself," interjected RK.

"You guys are right. My real name is Sayyed-Ul-Haq. I am from Bahawalpur. I was the former chief of Aafat-e-Ulfat and now reside here in India for over two years," said Sayyed with folded hands.

"Go on. We are listening. Explain the entire plan in sequence, from minor killings to water park mishaps and future plans, if any," an animated RK told Sayyed.

"I will cut a long story short and come to the point – A US company launched SUZI and made a deal with Doogle to enhance the experience. With this, they were unable to fulfill the orders. Hence, they proposed China for the job work and started manufacturing the units in Xiamen, a remote village in China."

"China? SUZI was manufactured in China? And nobody knew? How is that possible? Do you think this sounds trustworthy?" interrupted AK sir.

"Nobody should know. That's why SayTech chose a remote village. And once this deal was done, our organization saw this as an opportunity to destroy and disrupt India."

"How?" asked Shastri out of anxiety. And RK gave a warning through his eyes and gestured to Shastri to keep his mouth shut.

"Imraan-ul-Naved from the Independent China Terrorist (ICT) organization, which was residing in eastern China, was unhappy with the movement of Indian Armed forces at the Indo-China border. Also, your PM Mahendra Jain was trying to be over smart and took decisions which did not go well with many, and ICT was one of them."

"Wait a minute, you are hinting at THE ICT? The lethal and most dangerous terrorist organization in the world. Even they are in this with you?" asked a shocked AK.

"Yes," replied Sayyed with full certainty.

"FUCK! The entire world is against us," said AK and gestured to Sayyed to continue.

"So Imraan developed a contact at a very senior level in the company Xiamen Engineers, producing the device, SUZI.

After gaining confidence, the same company proposed software maintenance and better algorithm coding- to boost the functioning of the device, and at a price half than what they had already paid for the same services. Finley resisted initially as he had less confidence in China and its ethics, but somehow, he had to give it up against the other board of directors of SayTech, and the deal got sealed."

"Can I get some water, please?" requested Sayyed in the middle of everything.

"Give some water to this motherfucker. And you better not breathe after drinking water and continue until the end without any hiccups," ordered RK. He turned to Maatre to get water for him.

Maatre gave a glass of water and kept the jug filled with water right in front of Sayyed (just in case he needed more water). Sayyed drank thirstily and paused to breathe.

Looking at Sayyed, RK said ruthlessly, "I told you to be breathless and speak non-stop. We don't have an entire life to waste on you. Speak."

"So, we entered SayTech and Doogle territory, technically. The company got access to all the files. But there was a problem. Both companies had designed the cloud and the device program in such a way that nobody could access any file more than once, nor could they download anything from the cloud," added Sayyed.

"It is shocking to see that none of the companies sensed something dangerous coming their way and turned blind for extra income and profitability on paper," AK showed his disappointment at how things fell into a trap so easily.

"Somehow, our source found a weak point of Doogle, which was – Doogle had the maximum data sheet of all the people around the globe. They used to leak this data to various companies in different sectors like banks, telecom companies, loan companies, insurance companies, etc. In return, these companies used to fund various projects of Doogle, which made the company profitable (otherwise, it would be one of the major loss-making companies in the world)," added Sayyed.

"AK sir, this is the truth behind your Doogle being the biggest tech company in the world. You always felt proud of the company and wondered how we would survive without Doogle. No hard feelings, sir, but everything comes with a price tag, and it may not necessarily be in terms of money," taunted RK, looking at AK sir.

However, as ordered, Sayyed continued in a single breath, "This data further got leaked to non-reliable and fraudulent sources which carried out scams and earned crores. The catch was that a few of Doogle's employees helped these fraudsters by providing some technical services, which made these scams look real and genuine but, in reality, were fake. These funds were frequently routed through Doogle's fintech application and then channeled to the bank accounts of the fraudulent individuals and their accomplices. This created a vicious circle, which the ICT chief exploited to his advantage."

"How easy and normal it is for these companies to access our personal data. Advertisements show the data is encrypted and invisible. But the fact is, it's been leaked by the most trusted sources. How public is our personal life," Janhvi said with annoyance.

"The ICT chief got in touch with Doogle CEO Malti and presented the events taking place in the company. She resisted at first to give away security but later surrendered and gave access to the entire cloud system of Doogle when threatened about being exposed," continued Sayyed.

"And then you guys got in touch with SayTech CEO Finley and blackmailed him as they had a JV with Doogle. Out of fear and failure issues, SUZI and the entire application and software got compromised, and you started controlling SUZI," RK joined the dots of the story.

"Exactly," Sayyed agreed to RK's guess and confirmed it.

"Then you guys got access to all the devices installed around the globe. But you only targeted India and randomly picked the victims. But how did you guys blackmail them? We found absolutely nothing at any of the crime spots," AK further conjectured about the series of events.

"We downloaded videos of the kids, saved them to a pen drive, and personally delivered them to the victims when they were alone. We ensured the victims threw these pen-drives away a day before the crime and guided them on how to end their lives. We did so that no two crime scenes looked similar and no link was found," Sayyed gave closure to the first case of minor killings.

Everybody present had lost their cool and began to feel the entire episode was inhuman and insane. But Sayyed had no guilt or fear while describing the chapter, which fueled the fire and filled the CSTF unit with rage.

"The second one was easy. The flickering of lights, opening and shutting of doors, moving curtains, and all of that, which were application-based and connected with SUZI, were controlled by our source in China, and the ghost stories came up. And people turned crazy mad and turned for help, and I took advantage," added Sayyed, considering people's mindset being silly and having faith in supernatural forces.

"What was the purpose of setting up the manufacturing units?, questioned AK.

"Well, we trained the ones who participated in the robbery."

"What?" came in sync from the entire unit.

"Yes, we produced medicines during the day, and at night, we carried out base camps and trained the militants. The security in charge was paid a handsome salary to monitor the outside activity, and we carried our training inside. These security guards were told of banned drugs being processed for profits, but nobody knew about the actual doings."

"But how come every night these militants came in and left in the morning before the actual shift?" asked a bamboozled RK

"They were brought in by lorries and left in the morning by the same. As I already told you, the security guards were in a myth that these trucks carried the banned drugs," answered Sayyed with all smartness.

"Freaking hell. What planning you guys did! And nobody knew about the illegal training happening for months. Go on," said AK.

"Everybody was assigned a role, from keeping an eye to noticing the daily routine to making the plan work as decided and on schedule, and so on and so forth," said Sayyed.

"Then you guys marked the locations by opening the retail outlets and executed the plan as it unfolded," added RK to the story.

"Yes," Sayyed nodded.

"And finally, coming to the Waterpark tragedy, it was all controlled by the US, and no manpower was involved. The device SUZI, its application, the entire programming, and the software were installed at the water park. We just hindered its normal functioning and increased the electromagnetic fields, which led to the production of ions and electrization of water and, thus, the deaths. This is it," concluded Sayyed.

"And not to forget the looted gold and cash was used to fund the ICT. Even SayTech accepted the funds as they were helpless, so they thought it was good to at least make some money to benefit the company," added Sayyed.

The CSTF unit was emotional, and their eyes were moist. It was difficult to hold on to the tears, but somehow, they managed. It was not the time to mourn but to take revenge. The proof was right in front, and the team required the right planning to implement an equivalent disastrous riposte.

What the team heard from Sayyed's mouth and what the entire country went through in the last three years was unbelievable but true. Sayyed continued to be under supervision in the safe house. AK and RK planned a meeting with the higher authorities. They knew they had little time to act as they could not hold back Sayyed's unofficial arrest for long.

CHAPTER TEN

The Counter Plan

Two days after Sayyed's arrest, CAU and CSTF jointly requested the PMO to hold a meeting. They were assertive about their investigation and wanted to share it with the PM. The meeting got sanctioned, and on the day of the meeting –

In the conference room at the PMO –

"Welcome, everyone," greeted the PM.

"Per the request, we have kept this meeting very confidential. So, it will just be me, Home Minister Adiraj Pandey, Defense Minister Yugvendra Chauhan, and you, Akshay, and Ranbir. So let us begin."

"Certainly, sir," replied AK.

"Sir, I would like to bring to your notice something. We all know what happened in Splash 'N' Wet water resort. The local teams declared it a technical fault and shut the case, but we still went to double-check."

"But why?"

"Sir, we sensed something unusual in the case, and to our surprise, it proved true. We would like to connect this pen drive to the system and give a presentation with evidence on the projector. Ranbir will take over from here and explain further the proceedings."

Ranbir was unaware that he would have to put forward the evidence and gave a death stare to AK. He went speechless for a while.

"Mr. Ranbir, are we waiting for something? If not, please throw some light on the case," said Yugvendra sarcastically. Akshay got up, switched off the light, and turned on the projector.

"Sure, sir. Sorry. So, sirs, in our investigation, we found THE STA-SUZI to be the prime reason for the technical failure, which did not happen on its own. The device and the software were fabricated and hence the consequences."

"Ranbir, can you please elaborate," the PM asked enigmatically.

"Sir, as per the company SayTech, the device is meant to control infrared sensing, motion sensing, warning on anything unusual, or give an alarm in case of any technical fault. Even if it is malfunctioning, it can at the max shut down within no time and stop working totally," explained Ranbir about the technical working of the device with the demo on the projector.

"As per the claims made by the company and your presentation, Mr. Ranbir, it looks as if the tragedy was avoidable and controllable. Then what made it come down to this bad, rather its worst," asked the PM.

"Certainly, sir. But as I told you before, the working was fabricated, making the device over-perform. Look at the demo video carefully, sirs (Ranbir pointing towards the screen). This created an electromagnetic field, and ionization created a progressive current formation. Thus, the entire event was gradual – we first saw the increased formation of waves, then their intensity, and after a few hours, when the water got totally ionized, people died of shock." Ranbir showed the exact incident as it occurred by creating a replica video.

"So, you mean it was a controlled or rather planned uncontrolled failure that led to dire consequences," the PM questioned in surprise.

"Yes, and this is not all. As per my knowledge, either the software company has done it independently or has allowed some third-party access to its software and did what they did."

"But why would they allow any bug to enter the system? This could harm their future activities," asked the PM in confusion.

"Exactly, my point, sir. This leaves us with no option but to believe that the US is responsible for everything. This also brings me to a theory that they made you the guest of honor during the launch after the JV to win our confidence."

The theory took everyone by surprise.

"Also, this is not the end. The minor killings, the ghost news, and the robberies that happened were all planned and executed with the help of this device – SUZI."

"How can you be so sure? Can you please join the dots and complete all that has been initiated," the Home Minister AP, somewhat pissed, ordered the two.

"Sir, AK sir will take over."

"Thanks, Ranbir, that was unexpected. Sir, coming to the easiest part first – the robberies that took place at different places were planned. There were the Guru-Veda stores just adjacent to these shops and shared a common wall, which proves the target marking," explained AK by showing various evidence on the projector.

"And as per Ranbir's theory – they all had the device – SUZI installed at their shops and were down with connectivity problems simultaneously, which cannot be a coincidence. Also, PM sir, sorry to say, but all these locations were a part of the 'Smart India program,' continued AK.

"This proves the targets were out of those 300 cities installed with the application – SUZI and its software, as proposed by the US President."

"So you're hinting at Mr. Douglas being involved in the plan?" the worried PM asked AK.

"Well, sir, there are no clues on this, and I highly doubt it to be this way. I am sure Mr. President is unaware of the things in the same way we are and was just made a scapegoat at the launch event."

"Hmmm... All the servers are down simultaneously, and CCTV is not working within a radius of 5km. All of this proves Ranbir's theory to be true," replied PM appreciating Ranbir.

"Regarding the minor killings, we found that SUZI recorded the day-to-day activities at all places without the customer's consent or knowledge. In the first case, we found SUZI blackmailing Ziya with videos of her undressing, and hence, she ended her life out of fear."

"What?" AP reacted with shock.

"Yes, sir. In the second case of Mahi and Divya, it is a little sensitive, and I request that we keep it confidential so that we don't tarnish the image of the two."

"Akshay, we know the same, so need not worry," assured the PM.

"So, in the second case, these kids met regularly for studies. And when no one was around, they got a little bit intimate, which got recorded. When analyzed, we found the videos being stored in the cloud storage. The application again blackmailed the two, and the end result was the same."

"Finally, in the third case, the kids partied and consumed drugs, the videos of which…"

"Just hold on, Akshay, and stop," interrupted the PM.

"As I know, the cloud storage application must be huge. Because there were not one, two, or ten videos, but maybe thousands or more because so many kids were blackmailed. This could be our lead. Isn't it? The PM asked with some hope.

"Absolutely right, sir! So, this is where the situation gets more challenging. In this case, the someone is none other than Doogle, another company in the same country. This leads us to a more complex situation," replied AK hopelessly.

"I got you, AK, but now what? It is a clear case where SUZI is the murder weapon, and Doogle is the partner in crime. But there has to be someone who has controlled it from somewhere. Now, who is this someone, and how do we catch him?" the clueless Home Minister asked.

"One minute, Adiraj ji, why can we not present the proof from the storage and ask the US officials to do something about it? What do you have to say, members?" the PM again got a bit positive.

"I don't agree with this, sir. Sorry, but this is totally not the way this case should end. We will present the proof, they will withdraw the device, and tomorrow, bring something else that will again be the same or more lethal. This doesn't serve justice to whatever has happened in our country," Ranbir said angrily.

"Shut up, Ranbir, and sit down," AK ordered.

"NO, sir, I am not going to. Sir, we need to take revenge. We need to show them we are no less. Though we are moved by what happened, we are not shattered or scattered," Ranbir continued confidently.

"Sir, we need to find the cause behind this, and everybody in the room present knows that if we give up so easily, the incidents can be repeated. Sir, let's go for the kill, but humanly," explained a determined RK to all.

"And what is the plan, young man?" asked the PM to an infuriated RK.

"But sir, this is not the right approach," said a concerned Yugvendra.

"Well, let us hear the plan and then decide. I think RK is right, and we need to give away our typical image of being polite and show our real strength to the world," the PM replied.

"So, sir, we plan an attack on the US at Doogle's office. But we will not harm mankind. We will do what Mr. Bhagat Singh, the great Indian freedom fighter, did before his arrest. He attacked the parliament, but bombs were thrown at empty places with a clear intention to create fear and not harm mankind."

"And how do we do that? Is this some kind of a joke? My dear kid, you sound amateur. This is not a masala film," an animated Yugvendra asked.

"Sir, we plan an attack on Saturday on the corporate wing of Doogle, which remains shut. The same will create chaos in the entire campus, and thus, the situation will be as planned," continued Ranbir, turning a deaf ear to whatever the Defense Minister said.

"PM sir, how do you allow this man to share such a foolish plan? The plan is a total failure from the word go. If we try something like this, an inquiry will be sent on us rather than the US," Yugvendra said to the PM agitatedly.

"Can you please keep your mouth shut for a while, Yug? If you are not interested, then you may leave the room and wait for my orders," an enraged PM reprimanded Yugvendra.

"Sorry, sir."

"Ranbir, how do we do that? We can't do so by an air strike, bombing, or anything of that sort. We don't want to create any war-like situation," the PM sounded less confident this time.

Ranbir and AK looked at each other and smiled. Ranbir gestured for AK to take over, but he shook his head and asked Ranbir to continue further.

"What's up between you two? We are waiting for a plan. Please share," AP told the two, noticing their antics.

"Sure, sir. Sir, Sayyed-Ul-Haq will execute the plan," replied Ranbir with a huge smile.

"Who is this Sayyed now?" Yugvendra again interjected.

"Are you talking about Sayyed, from the Pakistani terror group who died in the plane crash?" asked the PM apprehensively.

"Yes, sir, our self-proclaimed 'GOOD ELEMENT' of society, Guru ji, aka Sayyed-Ul-Haq. He is not a saint but a well-trained militant from the terrorist group Aafat-e-Ulfat," Ranbir presented a shocker to everyone.

"What?" came in sync from all three ministers in the room. They looked frightened.

"Yes, sirs, you heard right. Remember the plane crash news from China that caught everyone's attention five years back?"

"Yes," replied the PM.

"The world was deeply saddened by the incident but also celebrated the death of the most wanted terrorist, Sayyed. But that was a mere cover for the plan," continued Ranbir.

"What plan?" intervened the Home Minister.

"Sir, he never boarded the flight and took the next flight to China in the name of Kazi Mohammad. The flight did not crash. Rather, it was a well-planned mass suicide that had only militants from Pakistan. These people created the balloon to cover Kazi, aka Sayyed's moves. Soon after landing, he took shelter in China for some time."

All of them were taken aback by the kind of planning the terror group did. They were petrified, tensed, and numb. The evidence and facts presented by the investigating team were indigestible but true.

"How come he entered India?" somehow, the PM managed to grunt.

"By land. From China, he crossed the western border and traveled to Uttarakhand unofficially. As planned, he remained underground for a few months in India and emerged as Guru ji from the Himalayan mountains, as he stated."

"Okay, all of this accepted, but why would a terrorist help India?" a confused Yugvendra asked Ranbir.

"Well, because we have forced him to turn hostile. We activated our agent network in Pakistan and learned about his family. Unfortunately, he has a large family of 32 members, all under the radar. They are monitored 24/7, and if he tries to be smart, we know what to do," intervened AK.

"So how and when do we proceed?" asked the PM with tension.

The entire plan's blueprint was presented and discussed. The situation didn't look good, and none of the ministers felt confident. Even RK and AK were nervous at the back of their mind. One wrong step would land them in big trouble. The attack was scheduled for 15th August, Independence Day.

"Ok, folks. It's time to free India again, albeit from technical terror. So, this 15th August, we shall see and breathe in new India. Though we have lost a lot in the last few years, we should see this as an opportunity to avoid further damage," concluded the PM and wished good luck to everyone present.

As AK and RK walked towards the exit, the PM asked them to wait. He gestured for the other ministers to leave.

"Good job, guys. But you could have taken me in confidence and made me a part of your plan," the PM smilingly told the two.

"Sorry, sir, we didn't get you," asked AK in confusion.

"C'mon, young man, I know you already had a plan, and this meeting was just for formal approval. Everything was pre-decided, and you two created false disarray by pitching against each other during Sayyed's topic," the PM patted the two with a cheeky smile.

AK and RK started to sweat in the air-conditioned room. They didn't expect the PM to know about this and turned speechless before the PM's intelligence.

"Relax, boys, it is ok, but remember one thing – just get the country free by hook or crook. If you need anything in the future regarding this, you can directly contact me." The PM then asked the two to leave.

AK and RK felt way more confident than before this meeting, as PM had shown immense faith in them and their plan.

CHAPTER ELEVEN

The Penultimate Execution

The sudden disappearance of Guru ji made the country go crazy. The followers could not connect, nor were they aware of his whereabouts. Also, the crowd could not doubt anyone, as Guru ji was kidnapped with utmost secrecy and kept at a safe house way beyond the common man's reach. Few believed that Guru ji had marched towards the Himalayas for meditation, while others still wondered about his sudden no-show decision.

Even the government officials decided to keep the arrest undisclosed, knowing that the announcement would create disorder. And this time, the officials were in no mood to take any chances.

While all this was happening, Sayyed, at the safe house, once again had to go under the knife to alter his appearance drastically, ensuring that he was totally unrecognizable. Sayyed's fake passport was made in the name of Asim Mehmood, giving him a new identity along with the makeover. And the team was all set for the action as planned.

15 days to the attack.

31ˢᵗ July, India.

As per the plan, five people headed toward Nepal as tourists. Four out of five were CSTF officers, and the fifth was Sayyed alias, Asim Mehmood. The group entered Nepal, crossing the Nepal-Bihar order via Darbhanga by road. The team spent two days wandering and enjoying the beautiful landscapes of Nepal, making sure they looked like tourists and nobody doubted them.

On the third day, the team contacted their source, an Indian agent – Ayesha Shaikh. From here on, Ayesha and Asim were supposed to take the mission ahead. The two posed as husband and wife and, the same night had a flight to America. The remaining officers planned to stay in Nepal for a few more days until the mission was completed.

Ayesha and Asim headed towards the airport, went through security checks without hitches, and soon boarded the flight. The flight took off and landed in America in sixteen hours. They were received by another Indian source, William Henry, and taken to his residence. Willy stayed with his wife, daughter, son, and mother. Asim was introduced as a friend he made during his visit to Nepal, and Ayesha, obviously his better half.

William Henry, aka Willy, was CEO and one of the board of directors at the helicopter-making company – Heli-Boeing Aircrafts. He was the head of the scrap department at Heli-Boeing, looking after the discarded helicopters and in charge of dismantling the old helicopters. The company made huge profits out of this, mainly standing positive on the balance sheet because of this arm of Heli-Boeing. Thus, Willy was one of the company's most trusted and dependent employees.

Fifteen Years Back – The Willy Connect

Willy had come in contact with Indian officials during his trip to India. On returning from a business meeting, Willy was drunk and driving. Under the influence of alcohol, he crashed his car and ran over four beggars sleeping on the streets. AK was the senior inspector then and handled this case. Willy was arrested immediately and put behind bars. The case was kept on a very low profile as a foreign citizen was involved.

None of them died in the accident, but all four were severely injured. Willy begged AK for his life and was ready to go to any extent to pay for his sins. AK went with his instinct and decided to retain Willy as an asset in America.

AK had to fight the system to induce his decision and butter many of his seniors. After much opposition, obstruction, and discrepancy, AK somehow managed to let Willy go. Before Willy left, he signed a statement agreeing to the accident. He was made to compensate the injured, and the receipts were kept as proof, and there was much more to the case to prove Willy guilty if ever he changed his mind someday.

But that never happened, and Willy always stayed loyal to India. He was always ready to serve for the good that the

Indians did for him. And after fifteen years, the time had come for Willy to repay.

The Present Day

Willy made a fake ID to get Asim to enter the scrap department of Heli-Boeing. Ayesha stayed home to monitor everything and ensure the mission went as decided. Asim was a trained militant who knew how to fly an aircraft in an emergency.

Asim was allotted a helicopter to check its efficiency. (All the helicopters went under several quality control tests before dismantling. This helped to distinguish the useful and useless parts of the aircraft). Every day, Asim spent hours in an abandoned helicopter and polished his skills of taking off, controlling, landing, and all that was required. Willy frequently visited Asim to check his progress and clear any doubts.

Two days before the attack –

Ayesha calls AK (at CSTF headquarters) through secured lines with the utmost care, "We are good to go, Chief. Things seem on track. Asim is set to go."

"I am sure, Ayesha," came a reply from AK in a dejected tone.

"Sir, you sound very low. Are you fine? Is the situation under control there?" asked a worried Ayesha.

"All is well here. It's just that I am nervous. Very nervous. I have high hopes, and others have bet on me and my operation.

Even then (referring to the Willy incident), they showed immense faith in me and let him go. It is time to repay and do something for the country," a nervous AK replied.

"Sir, all will be good; have faith in God. You have done your part and have been successful to date. Now don't let this affect you, especially when it is no more in your hands," Ayesha tried to infuse some confidence in AK.

"You are right, Ayesha, but don't forget, I am in charge of this mission. And God forbid, if anything goes out of track or comes to a situation that is uncontrollable or cannot be handled, then it will be me who will be responsible and not Willy, Asim, you, or anyone associated with this."

"Sir, let us be positive and not think of things going wrong. We will do it and celebrate the day after. This will be my final call, and after this, you will see or hear from the news on the decided day," continued Ayesha courageously.

"Sure. Just give my message to Asim. Kabir is still watching his family. Even the smallest of mistakes, and he will see the consequences for himself," said AK sternly and ended the call.

AK headed towards Ranbir's cabin.

Knocking at the cabin door, "Hey, Ranbir, busy? May I come in? Can we have a quick chat?"

Looking at AK, RK says, "Not at all, sir. Please come in. You don't need to ask me before entering, sir," Ranbir smiled and invited AK sir to sit.

"Thanks, Ranbir. Ayesha called from America. We are all set to go. Things are on track, and everything looks good till now," AK said.

"That's good news, sir. Now let's keep our fingers crossed and wait for the results," RK said, slightly nervous.

There was silence in the room for a minute. AK didn't leave even after sharing the news. Looking at this, an anxious Ranbir asked, "Sir, everything alright? Is there anything else that you wish to share?"

"Yes, I will come straight to the point. I am sorry we have had differences during the case, and I often crossed my limits. I should not have said things that I did in the past. So I am sorry again and hope you don't harbor any grudges," AK said guiltily, seeming to ask forgiveness.

On hearing this, Ranbir got up, came close to AK sir, and said, "Sir, you are my senior, and I respect everything you said. You are more experienced and may have had ideas for handling the situation per the rules. I am a bit impulsive and believe in prompt action. Our working methods might differ, but we always had the same goal. So, sir, please don't feel guilty."

"For sure, we have had the same goals, which should be achieved soon," replied AK sir confidently and left the room.

The Day Before the Attack

Willy meets his friend James, the owner of a scrapyard company dealing in all types of scrap material, from cars to aircraft. In advance, some two weeks back, Willy informed James to provide him a helicopter in the best possible flying condition and asked him to keep it a secret.

James was reluctant to do the job for Willy, but he was offered an amount he could not have earned even by dismantling hundreds of sports cars. Also, Willy had good contacts in the government and promised James the next tender from 'The American Scrap Association' for his company. The tender coming to James' company meant the profits would double for the year, so James could not deny Willy anything.

On meeting Willy, he said, "Hey buddy, this has to be kept under wraps. No one should know I have helped you. And who is this guy? I have never seen him before," asked James, looking at Asim.

"He is a friend from Nepal, Asim. And not to worry, our lips will be zip-locked, and no one will ever know about this deal. But where is the machine?" asked Willy, looking around.

"Willy, I am not a fool to call you here in my company and hand over the helicopter. Let's go to the countryside. I have my row house. It's parked there. Also, there is an open space where all the quality checks can be carried out easily."

The three of them got in the car. James headed to the countryside. He kept driving for an hour and a half, but the place could not be seen. Willy and Asim looked frustrated, kept checking their wristwatches, and felt the time was wasted, but they were helpless.

Finally, after a drive of two and a half hours and covering a distance of more than 100 miles, they arrived at their destination. The place was extremely remote and in the middle of the forest. It was not a row house, as James informed the two, but rather a palace spread over almost an acre.

Willy and Asim were shocked to see the beautiful mansion and wondered what James did there. The three got out of the car. "Come guys, let's go in and check the machine," signaled James, asking them to follow.

Both followed James and were baffled, looking at the interior of the palace. It looked bigger from the inside and luxurious. A small electric vehicle was parked at the entrance. James invited Willy and Asim to sit with him, and the three traveled in opposite direction.

They reached the extreme end and, through a small door, exited the helipad area at the back of the palace on the other end. James removed the cover and unveiled the chopper. The chopper looked fine from the outside. All three got in the helicopter, did the quality checks, and were satisfied with the results.

"Let's check the engine, flying capacity, and all of that," Willy said to Asim, to which Asim nodded.

"Wait, hold on for a second. Is Asim the pilot? He doesn't look like one to me. Will he be able to control the copter?" interrupted James.

Asim came to the pilot's seat, took position, and was ready to take off. "Hey Asim, tell me, are you the pilot?" asked James again doubtfully. When Asim didn't reply, James turned to Willy, "This man doesn't speak; is he dumb? Hey Willy, what's going on? Even you are mum. C'mon man, I need to know this," James stopped Asim from taking off.

"Look, James, I have paid you for the chopper, and I can do whatever I wish with this. You can get out of the copter if you have doubts about him being the pilot, but I request you not to frustrate us any further," Willy replied angrily.

"Oh, surely I will get down, but this is my house, and you need to know that," James said in a firm tone and got out of the helicopter. He stood about 200 feet and witnessed the take-off.

Asim started the engine, and Willy sat next to him. The rotor blades spun, and the rotating wings produced the necessary airflow. The airflow gradually increased and produced a lift when it reached the maximum. The helicopter rose about a foot, and suddenly, the entire system stopped. 'Dhudum' came the noise, and the helicopter was back to its place.

James was horrified seeing this, and his belief of Asim not being a trained pilot doubled. He began to approach the chopper when suddenly the engine started again, the airflow reached the max levels, and the helicopter took off. Willy and Asim took a test flight and soon returned. The two appeared contented with the working of the chopper's mechanism.

Willy shook hands with James. "James, the chopper looks good, and we are happy."

"To hell with you guys. He is not a trained pilot, for sure. If he tried flying the copter, it would not cover much distance and crash soon. It's unbelievable, Willy. I helped you with this. You are risking lives by betting on his skills. And tell me one thing, why he doesn't speak?" an angry James yelled at the two for their antics.

"James, Asim is a retired pilot. He has flown in five years and tried his skills today. Relax. He will not harm anyone. Coming to him not talking, he is the same with everyone," Willy tried to calm James down.

"I don't care what you do with this man and the chopper. Just remember – my name should not surface anywhere in all of this. Also, where do you want me to transport the chopper?" asked James to get rid of the chopper and the two idiots at the earliest.

Willy took his mobile out of his pocket to check the target's distance from the countryside. He typed the location on the navigation map, showing about 200 miles. Willy, in his mind – the machine could cover a distance of 350 miles. Even if it was not in the best condition, the efficiency would reduce to 250 miles. This meant they still had the buffer fuel for 50 miles in the worst-case scenario.

"Let the helicopter be here. We will take off from here tomorrow morning sharp at 10.00 hours. We will stay here for the night if you don't mind and leave in the morning," replied Willy after calculating everything.

"Well, I don't mind you guys staying, but the problem is you guys will have to help yourself as I won't be staying back. Also, there isn't anything to eat, so stay hungry and stay happy. May God bless you in this jungle," James replied with a wicked smile.

The fear of being alone in the jungle with no food gripped the two, but Willy and Asim had no other option. Transporting the chopper from the palace to another place for take-off was difficult and risky. They found the option of staying back the best and gave a fake thumbs-up to James.

"Lock the door when you leave tomorrow. Don't worry. It's automated with SUZI. Take care until we meet next if you guys are alive," James left.

Willy immediately called Ayehsa after James's departure, and he informed her about the situation.

"What? I must be present, Willy, when Asim leaves for the mission. Why the hell you don't understand he is my responsibility here," scolded Ayesha over the call.

"Well, Ayesha, I know what you say, but this was the best we could think of. Also, the target is just 200 miles from here, and this place is away from the crowd, which makes it even safer for a hide-out," convinced Willy.

"Ok! Send me the location, and I shall be there soon."

"Ayesha, get some food along. We have nothing to eat and more than half a day to spend," pleaded Willy.

"Sure." Ayesha ended the call.

Ayesha packed her bag, kept the laptop and some snacks to munch, and left. She took almost 3 hours to reach and was equally amazed as the two when she reached the palace. She saw the helicopter and had a smile on her face with a thought at the back of her mind that, finally, she could sense the mission had begun from this moment.

The Day of the Attack, 15th August

Morning 7 A.M.

Ayesha went to Asim's room to wake him up and found him already awake. He was standing near the window and gazing at the sun. He looked expressionless.

"It's time, Asim, to get going. Let us discuss the plan one final time and then get ready for action," Ayesha said, standing at the door.

"I know what I have to do. Please don't bore me with the plan again. We have discussed this more than a hundred times, but not anymore. I beg you to let me spend this time alone and remember my family one last time. Because after this, I am unsure if I will be left alive," a frustrated, weak Asim begged Ayesha for some 'me' time.

"You at least know you have to die. People who lost their lives in India because of you didn't even know they were breathing their last breath. Even they had families and few dreams, had they known their end was near, they would have done the same as you do today. Well, this is the difference between a militant and an officer: both have guns, but we know when to pull the trigger. Take your time, and I shall visit you again afterward," replied Ayesha with a heavy heart and moist eyes.

For once, Asim had tears in his eyes, whether from guilt or missing his family, but he turned emotional after hearing Ayesha. He kept looking outside the window with those moist eyes.

After spending an hour with himself, Asim prayed and soon got ready. He came out of the room and walked towards the common area of the palace where Ayesha and Willy were already present.

Looking at Asim, Willy says, "So, Asim, this is it. From here on, you are on your own. You know what and how of the plan. I need not repeat or tell you. Don't try to act smart at any point. Kabir is present right outside your house." Willy gives a pat on Asim's back.

Ayesha takes a gun-like tool from her bag and asks Asim to extend his left hand, "Quick."

"But why? What is this, and what is it for? I am doing as I have been told. Then what kind of gunshot is this?" questioned a scared Asim.

"I will insert a chip through this gunshot to track you. Also, it is equipped with sound sensor technology, which will update me about the explosion. It triggers only with the decibels of high levels like that of a blast or something." Ayesha pulled his hand forward.

Asim was scared and reluctant but somehow took the shot in his arm and was ready to leave. Soon, the three headed towards the helipad. Asim took the position in the cockpit, buckled himself, and was all set to go. Willy went inside the helicopter, checked the mechanisms again, and returned.

Ayesha and Willy signaled that it was good to go, and with this, Asim started the engine. The blades began to rotate and gradually caught speed. The fan moved full force, and the helicopter rose from the ground. Within seconds, it took off in full swing.

Asim headed towards the target and was being tracked constantly by Ayesha.

At the same time, India.

The entire CSTF and CAU team gathered at the CSTF headquarters. Nobody was on the field, nor were they working on anything. Today was just a wait-and-watch day for all. They were in constant touch with the PM at Red Fort in Delhi to celebrate Independence Day. The atmosphere was tense, and anxiety was evident on each individual's face.

In America

Asim traveled at full speed towards the target and was just 50 miles away. Ayesha and Willy were nervous; their hearts pumped at double the speed, and their heartbeats intensified further as he approached the target.

Finally, 10 miles from the target, Asim locked the target – the corporate wing of Doogle, as decided, put the helicopter into autopilot mode and was ejected off the seat. Asim wore the parachute jacket, and as the helicopter entered the Doogle premises, he jumped off the helicopter.

Ayesha and Willy kept track of Asim as he reached the target. The tracker had covered more than 190 miles and suddenly stopped moving. Soon, in 5, 4, 3, 2, and 1, the helicopter crashed right in the middle of the corporate wing of Doogle. There was a huge blast that shook the entire Doogle campus. The building was made of glass, and its pieces flew hundreds of meters. The entire building caught fire quickly, and the other far-off Doogle wings began to evacuate.

The situation turned bizarre, and there was a stampede on the campus. The employees, security personnel, and everyone present ran for their lives. The scenario was similar to that seen in the water park tragedy, but none losing their lives (until now) was the major difference.

Soon, the firemen arrived due to a fire alarm installed at the campus. They, in turn, called the police. The police came in full force in no time and transferred people to a safer place outside the campus. The buses arrived, picked up the people transferred outside the campus, and took them to another location.

The ambulances waiting outside treated the injured people on the spot. And very few had major injuries and were taken to hospitals. Shortly, the media arrived and started the live coverage of everything happening. Soon, the entire mishap was live and reached the television sets of CSTF headquarters and the world.

In the middle of the chaotic situation, Asim stood calm under a tree at the campus entrance and appeared numb. He neither moved nor approached anyone. Soon, a policeman spotted Asim and found it weird that he was not running for his life. The same police personnel approached Asim, and as decided, Asim surrendered.

It took hours to bring the situation under control and rescue the present staff. The good news was nobody lost their life during the course, and very few were severely injured.

At the CSTF Headquarters in India

The entire unit celebrated the blast. Though they knew it was sadistic, they were happy they did not kill the innocent. AK sir congratulated Ranbir on his mission accomplishment and hugged him. Soon, AK called the PM and gave him the news. His happiness knew no limits.

The Interrogation

The Next Day

Asim was handed over to the top investigating body in America – the Crime Control Bureau (CCB). No one knew why Asim surrendered and his motive behind the crash. Moreover, the Americans were surprised by the very fact that he did not harm mankind.

Mr. Carlos Rutherford, the head of CCB, arrived at the CCB headquarters and, without any delay, went ahead with the interrogation. The entire suspense created was about to unfold in the most unlikely manner, and in a way the Americans would have never imagined.

"What is your name?" asked Carlos angrily.

"Sayyed-Ul-Haq," came the fearless reply.

"Sayyed. Who Sayyed? And why did you crash land at the Doogle? We did the necessary examination of the helicopter, and the results showed no technical failure. So tell me the exact reason because the American Government is behind my ass, and I have a lot of pressure from the technical giant Doogle. So no-nonsense and speak only what makes sense," Carlos threatened Sayyed, holding him by his neck.

"Sayyed-Ul-Haq, former Chief of Aafat-e-Ulfat, a terrorist organization in Pakistan. The most wanted man on earth, I am the same man – Sayyed. So leave my neck and stay within your limits. You never know; the next target might be this building," Sayyed warned Carlos.

As soon as he introduced himself as Sayyed, Carlos walked out of the room and asked one of the officers to look for Sayyed's history and verify the truth in the claims. And soon after, Carlos got back with the interrogation. After some time, an officer came into the room, whispered something to Carlos, handed over a file to him, and left.

"So you are Sayyed, right? Then why the hell is the name on the Pakistani passport, Asim Mehmood? And I have got Sayyed's photo with me, and he nowhere resembles you. Stop blabbering shit and come straight to the point," said Carlos losing his patience.

"I have come from India just to attack you. You can call the Indian government and ask for the same."

After a short pause, Sayyed says, "Wait a minute, there is a chip in my body. You can remove and scan it. A few of your questions will be answered automatically."

Carlos called the technical team. He asked them to take Sayyed to the examination room and check for the chip. The team took Sayyed along with them and scanned him. Surprisingly, they found the tracker in his body and removed it by making a small incision in his forearm.

An officer came running to Carlos in the room along with the chip, "Sir, we found this in his body. He was telling the truth," said the officer, showing the chip to Carlos.

"Send this to the laboratory for testing immediately and ask them to be quick, keeping everything else aside. I want the results by the end of this day and shall proceed further with the interrogation only after the reports are out. Also, put that man in lock-up for now," ordered Carlos.

The officer left and followed the instructions. In the meantime, half the CCB officers formed a search party to trace the location of Asim's (as mentioned in the passport) residence in America. The rest of the unit at the CCB headquarters studied the history of the most wanted man and landed with the story of Sayyed's end in the plane crash.

Carlos was updated about all the progress in the case and was informed of everything they found about Sayyed. Carlos believed every bit, but that the mystery person in his jail was speaking the truth about having a chip in the body did not go well. He felt some truth in the man's story.

The day passed, and around 8 p.m. came the reports, and to his shock, Carlos found that the man had been telling the truth about him being from India. That was not it. The chip was not just a tracker but also a memory card with a video of Guru ji undergoing surgery to change the look. It was done in the safe house before the initiation of the operation.

"Get me Sayyed immediately," ordered Carlos to the officer who got the reports to him.

Sayyed saw Carlos holding the chip in one hand and its report in the other. With a cheeky smile, Sayyed said, "Carlos, you appear helpless to me. Is everything alright? Or is there anything I can help you with?"

"I am shaken and got to believe in your story. Start from the beginning and do not stop until it's done," ordered Carlos.

Sayyed unfolded the mystery, starting with his early days as the AEU Chief, followed by how the ICT chief got in touch with the US tech companies – SayTech and Doogle. He continued with how his fake death was planned with the help of the Chinese government, followed by his entry into India as Guru ji and all the adversities he, along with his organization, implemented.

Carlos went speechless and was unable to digest everything presented to him. With the episodes unfolding, he understood the case was way bigger than what he approximated, and it was time for him to involve the government officials to decide further. Companies like SayTech and Doogle, who were involved in this terror, came as the biggest shocker to the CCB team.

Carlos contacted the official members of THE UNITED STATES DEPARTMENT of DEFENSE (USDOD). He convinced the officials to fix his meeting with the head of USDOD, Mr. Charlie Kennedy.

At the USDOD Headquarters

Carlos reached the headquarters the next day morning at 9 a.m.

"May I come in, sir," Carlos asked for permission, standing at the door.

"Carlos, please come in. So good to see you after a very long time. Carlos, you just have 10 minutes to brief me about the case. I have a meeting with Mr. President this afternoon and must prepare the pointers with my assistant. So your time starts now," replied Mr. Charlie in all his jolly mood.

"Sure, sir," Carlos disclosed everything about the findings in the case. Ten minutes passed in a jiffy, and still, Mr. Charlie didn't stop Carlos from speaking, as Charlie had realized the severity of the case. After almost an hour, Carlos finished talking, but Charlie didn't react and appeared completely lost.

"Sir, waiting for your reply," Carlos raised his voice and tapped his hand.

"Oh yes, Carlos. I don't know what to say. This is very serious. I think first and foremost we need to connect the Indian officials and know what they want," replied Charlie in a sunken voice.

"Perfect, sir, sounds good. How do we proceed?" questioned Carlos.

Looking at his wristwatch, he replied, "It is not too late. Let us connect with India over a call right away. I think connecting with my counterpart, the Defense Minister, Mr. Yugvendra, will be the best option for now. Let's see what he has to offer, or at least he will guide us through this."

Charlie immediately picked up the phone on his table, called the receptionist outside, and asked her to connect to Mr. Yugvendra in India. The call got connected.

"Hey Yug, my friend, how are you? Long time since we did not chat, so I thought of getting in touch with you," greeted Charlie over the call.

"Hello, Mr. Charlie. I am surprised to hear from you suddenly. Is everything alright? You also sound a bit different than usual," came a reply from Yug on the other side of the call.

"C'mon Yug, I expect you not to pretend and come straight to the point. I know you guys have attacked…"

"Hold on for a second. I will patch you through a secure line to my investigating body, and then we shall proceed. Rather, let us get connected on a video conference and discuss the matter further," interjected Yug.

"Okay."

Yug connected over a video call with the CSTF primarily.

"Sir, there is an incoming video call from the Defense Minister," informed Janhvi to RK.

"Get him online and inform AK, sir, he is out on the field for some work. Americans are ready for negotiations; we might also see them over call soon. Pick up, and let's get going," a hopeful RK replied.

On connecting over video call with Ranbir, the Defense Minister says, "Hello Ranbir, the American counterpart is waiting to connect with us and want to initiate the dialogue. I am patching you along. Let's get to the final step of the operation and finish it once and for all."

The three connect over a video call, and the dialogue begins –

"Hello, officer, so we will come straight to the point. What do you guys want us to do?" asks Charlie to Ranbir.

"Well, sir, with all due respect, we want you to suspend SayTech and Doogle services indefinitely unless we come to a mutual solution. Also, we will prepare an agreement mentioning how SayTech and Doogle helped the terrorist organization, and you will sign the same," replied Ranbir fearlessly.

"Mr. Yugvendra, this sounds amateur. We cannot sign any agreement; it will be like signing a suicide note. This is not possible; this is way too much. Mr. President will never agree on this," replied Charlie furiously.

"Sorry, Mr. Charlie, but the officer is not requesting, rather demanding. Talking of the agreement, don't worry. There will be a non-disclosure clause that will bind us from disclosing your involvement to the world until you are loyal. We have seen more than 250 suicides in the last three years, and more than 5,000 people have died. I think these numbers will be enough to convince your President," replied Yugvendra.

Hearing this, Charlie nodded and agreed without asking any questions. Yugvendra placed a few more conditions to seek justice for the country. Charlie heard the demands put by the Indians and requested a day to have a conversation with Mr. President and promised to get back.

Charlie met Mr. President the same afternoon as scheduled, but the agenda of the meeting changed. He briefed the President on the entire conversation with the Indian Defense Minister. On hearing about the events in India in the last few years, he asked to help India in every possible way.

Charlie connected with his counterpart in India the next day and was ready to act as the Indian Government desired.

CHAPTER TWELVE

The Final Showdown

The American Government created a false backdated history and story for Doogle being involved in various kinds of scams (which was true but were unaware of) and suspended the license immediately. The senior management of the company was put behind bars.

A press conference was held by the CCB officials, stating that the reason behind the attack at Doogle was a fraud with a (psycho) common man (whose identity was not disclosed) who lost all his savings during the course. And they made it look factual by justifying that the attacker only intended to harm the company and not mankind.

SayTech was asked to recall all the devices from all over the world at the earliest. This would mean a setback to the company, leading to more than a trillion-dollar loss and shutting down the company shortly. Soon after this, an agreement was signed between India and USA.

The former part of the condition was fulfilled, but the major part was still awaited. Indians were hopeful of getting what they deserved, as the American President stood tall beside them during all of this, and that too unconditionally.

23rd August, 10 A.M.

President's Office –

"Sir, we are ready with our jets and missiles. All the targets have been identified and locked. I still feel this is risky and might have repercussions. Are you sure we proceed as planned, or can we look for an alternative?" asked Charlie nervously.

"Did I just hear an alternative? We are the strongest country and biggest superpower globally and cannot help the terrorists. Though not directly, we did indirectly. And what if the Indians disclose the same? There is no alternative. India is our dear friend and the next superpower in the coming years. We cannot afford to lose Indian confidence if we have to achieve our goals," scolded the President.

"Sorry, sir," apologized Charlie.

"Get your men ready. Get the army ready. We attack as planned at 16.00 hours sharp," commanded Mr. President.

"Sir." Charlie left for the base camp, where the entire setup was readied for the attack.

Charlie reached the base camp in half an hour. On reaching the camp, the army chief, Mr. Justin Luther, paid a visit to Charlie.

"So, Mr. Luther, are we good to go? Are your boys ready?" asked Charlie.

"Sir, we are all set and waiting for your signal. I will just brief you on the plan in a flash. Post that, I would appeal to you to meet the boys heading for the mission, just to boost their confidence, only if you don't mind," requested Luther.

"Absolutely, we shall go and meet them," replied Charlie, patting Luther's back.

Luther started discussing the Plan of Action with Charlie. He showed him the targets on the projector and gave a demo of how they would attack and the damage it would cause. It looked good, and Charlie gave a thumbs-up to the perfect plan and hoped it went as Luther showed.

After the discussion, Charlie and Luther headed where the boys were waiting on the ground just before the take-off. Charlie requested if he could visit inside one of the fighter planes before he could talk to the boys. Luther agreed and took him for the demo.

Upon completing the demo, Charlie addressed the boys with full energy and confidence, "Boys, you know what you have to do. This is to teach the bastards a lesson, who have disturbed the equilibrium of society and harmed humanity. Let us go for the kill, but remember – you are precious and should return without fail."

"Sure, sir," came the echo from more than 100 officers present.

Everyone waited with bated breath. As the time neared, the thumping of the heart got heavier and heavier. The plan was not revealed to anyone. It was kept under wraps and private even to the UNITED NATIONS (the intergovernmental body responsible for maintaining international peace and harmony between the nations).

Action

At 15.30 hours, the time came to proceed with the mission. Charlie called Mr. President for permission one last time –

"Sir, we are good to go. Shall we proceed?" asked Charlie

"Good luck, Charlie," Mr. President said and disconnected. Charlie signaled a go-ahead to Mr. Luther.

"Ok, boys, start preparing and take positions. We fly at 16.00 hours exactly, right after 20 minutes. Remember one thing – attack, conquer, and return. Did you get that, boys?" asked Luther with full enthusiasm.

"Yes, Chief," replied the boys in sync with equal confidence.

"I cannot hear you. Higher with more power, repeat after me: Attack, Conquer, and Return," ordered Luther, infusing more energy in the boys.

"Attack, Conquer, Return, sir," replied the boys with conviction.

"Great. Move, move boys, and take position fast," said the chief.

With this, the final movement began. The boys headed towards different fighter planes. Charlie looked a bit nervous, whereas Luther was pumped. The boys had taken their seats and were stationed in the jet. They signaled all okay by giving thumbs-up.

Final checks with the Air traffic controller (ATC) were on. The runway was being checked and was set for the take-off. ATC gave clearance, and a man on the runway with a green flag, dropped it to give a go-ahead signal. The jet engines were on. Fifty jets were arranged for the attack at full capacity and lined up one behind the other.

The first jet covered the runway and took off, followed by the second, the third, and so on. The entire army of jets took off and headed in a group of 25 each, in two different directions for two locations.

Meanwhile, a few officers were stationed in the missile control room to attack the targets simultaneously as the jets. The entire movement of both units was also closely monitored from the control room.

Six hours after the take-off, one unit had reached Pakistan and the other China. They entered the air-path of both countries – one hovered above Aafat-e-Ulfat headquarters and the other over the ICT headquarters in China.

Surely, both countries must have got the infringement signals from their respective satellites, but before they could react – BOOM! The first bomb was dropped on the target at both locations. The missile was activated and left for the target. And after that first bomb, a series of bombs were dropped on Pakistan and China.

The scene was very animated and looked like bombs raining from the sky. Missile bombing accompanied, and this continued for the next sixty minutes. As soon as the target was achieved, the fighter planes returned to the USA base camp.

Apart from the terrorist organization, thousands lost lives as collateral damage. The entire city was destroyed, and barely any human was left alive. The scene was devastating and disturbing.

The fighter jets returned to the base in America, safe and secure. Each one heaved a sigh of relief. They smiled, clapped, hugged, and congratulated each other for success. Charlie congratulated Luther and informed the President.

India got the news of the attack from the media. Finally, justice was served. The entire unit got emotional and had moist eyes while they celebrated. The CSTF unit also felt bad for innocent people who died in China and Pakistan. But this is how it was meant to be. It was impossible to finish the terror without harming the surroundings.

The media blamed the Americans, but came the official statement from the horse's mouth, Sayyed himself.

"I am Sayyed-Ul-Haq, former chief of AEU who attacked the Doogle premises. This was just a test attack, and we were planning many attacks all around the globe along with the terrorist organization ICT. Our prime targets were India and America, but somehow, I was caught and had to disclose the plan."

After hearing the statement, the UN head, Mr. George Garland, warned the American Government and left them unpunished. The UN imposed various kinds of bans on Pakistan and China. They declared the two as threat nations to the world. Import and export were banned in both countries, and the economies of both nations went for a toss.

Again, amid all this, the one who suffered the most was the common man, but he did not have a choice. The common man is always left choiceless in all cases and is barely happy with any decisions.

While on the other hand, India was happy as everything went smoothly as planned. All the cases were closed, stating them unsolved officially, but unofficially, these cases were solved faster than the others. Each individual from CSTF was promoted to higher ranks, and the unit became dormant with a wish to never get activated again.

Akshay Kewadia, Ranbir Khandelwal, and Diler Khatri were awarded the highest gallantry awards. Diler's dream of 'The KKK' came true, and there were smiles all around.

The Conclusion

Man made technology for efficient working but progressed so much that they manually stopped working. We saw the gradual rise of SUZI, which affected relationships, economic balance, emotions, and productivity, and finally led to a technical war, which in turn led to a human war.

We need to gain control of devices and not let the device control us. Otherwise, the next world war may occur sooner or later for technical reasons.

THE END… or a new BEGINNING…